"I'm

thin...

Excep...
with k...

Right now, she couldn't bring herself to care about playing pool. She wanted Gray's mouth on her, his hands on her. Since she couldn't seem to find her voice, she met his eyes, confident that the longing she felt was clear in her expression.

Even though it had only been hours since they'd encountered each other at the office, it felt as if she'd been waiting forever for him to kiss her. His mouth settled over hers, and she parted her lips in invitation. She buried her fingers in his hair, surprised at how silky it was. Their kiss was salty and spicy, and her body pulsed with sensation.

Gray kissed the same way he shot pool, with bold assurance and innate skill. His possessiveness nearly made her moan, and he pulled back, teasing, nipping at her lower lip. She was glad she was balanced between him and the pool table. Despite her mocking his earlier boast that he made her weak in the knees, the longer he kissed her, the less steady she felt.

Lifting his head, he reached for the eight ball on the table and swiped it into a pocket. "Oops." His breathing was rapid, his voice strained. "Guess I lose. Ready to get out of here?"

Wordlessly, she nodded. If she were any more ready, they'd be arrested for public indecency.

Dear Reader,

Like the characters in this book, I live in the Atlanta area. One of my favorite things to do here is attend plays at the always entertaining Shakespeare Tavern. Since I'm a fan of Shakespeare's mistaken-identity comedies, it's fitting that my first book for Harlequin Blaze is a The Wrong Bed story.

On the day of her would-be wedding, Danica Yates decides that instead of brooding over her ex-fiancé's recent elopement, she'll celebrate her newfound freedom. By seducing the hot architect who works in her office building.

Her plan works great—except that she unknowingly propositions the architect's twin brother.

Aside from being physically identical, Sean Grayson is nothing like his studious, workaholic twin. Sean is impulsive with a track record of being just a bit wild. When a sexy brunette asks him to help her forget that it was supposed to be her wedding day, Sean can't resist saying yes.

But before the night is over, Sean starts to realize Dani may be his perfect match. How can he convince her they should have a real relationship—especially once she learns he hasn't been completely honest about his identity?

I hope you have as much fun reading my Harlequin Blaze debut as I did writing it. Look me up on Twitter (@TanyaMichaels) or facebook.com/AuthorTanyaMichaels and let me know what you think!

Best,

Tanya

New York Times Bestselling Author

Tanya Michaels

Good with His Hands

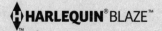

Recycling programs
for this product may
not exist in your area.

ISBN-13: 978-0-373-79845-2

Good with His Hands

Copyright © 2015 by Tanya Michna

Printed in U.S.A.

Tanya Michaels, a *New York Times* bestselling author and five-time RITA® Award nominee, has been writing love stories since middle school algebra class (which probably explains her math grades). Her books, praised for their poignancy and humor, have received awards from readers and reviewers alike. Tanya is an active member of Romance Writers of America and a frequent public speaker. She lives outside Atlanta with her very supportive husband, two highly imaginative kids and a bichon frise who thinks she's the center of the universe.

Books by Tanya Michaels
HARLEQUIN AMERICAN ROMANCE

The Best Man in Texas
Texas Baby
His Valentine Surprise
A Mother's Homecoming
"Hill Country Cupid" *in My Cowboy Valentine*

Hill Country Heroes Series

Claimed by a Cowboy
Tamed by a Texan
Rescued by a Ranger

The Colorado Cades Series

Her Secret, His Baby
Second Chance Christmas
Her Cowboy Hero

Texas Rodeo Barons Series

The Texan's Christmas

To get the inside scoop on Harlequin Blaze and its talented writers, be sure to check out blazeauthors.com.

All backlist available in ebook format.

Visit the Author Profile page at Harlequin.com for more titles.

Thanks to Harlequin editors Kathleen Scheibling
and Johanna Raisanen for welcoming me to Blaze
and to writer Lila Bell for the timely reminder of
how exhilarating it can be to try something new.

1

As a REAL-ESTATE AGENT, Danica Yates couldn't live without her cell phone. Clients and potential clients called at all hours to ask questions, make counteroffers and set up meeting times. But, so help her, if one more person texted another pitying variation of "How are you holding up?" Dani was going to run over the damn phone with her car.

For her smartphone's sake, she hurried through the parking lot, away from looming vehicular phonicide and toward the relative safety of her office building. More well-meaning texts and calls were inevitable. She'd already fielded a few in the weeks since her broken engagement, but just as the people in her life were beginning to drop the subject, Tate had made his big social-media announcement last night, spurring more unwanted sympathy.

Grimly hoping that Tate Malcom's hairline would recede and his man parts wither, she dropped her phone into the pocket of her lightweight trench coat. Spring in Atlanta was fickle. This particular Wednesday morning, it was only ten degrees above freezing, but by afternoon, she'd probably be coatless and running the air-conditioning in her car.

As she passed a row of blooming Bradford pear trees, the heels of her boots clicked decisively against the pavement. She loved the black leather boots and their defiant three-inch heels. After Tate's self-deprecating jokes about her "towering" over him—she was five-ten to his five-nine— she'd mostly worn flats during their relationship.

Well, screw that. She hadn't straightened her hair since their breakup, either, abandoning the sleeker look for dark brown corkscrew curls that fell halfway down her back, adding extra volume and height. Reaching for the front door, she took a moment to reassure herself that the woman reflected in the glass didn't look jilted and pathetic. *You are determined and successful and you will be far too busy today to spare that worm Tate another thought.*

First, she was going to stop by the coffee place on the first floor for a much-needed chai latte. Then, with her mind sharpened by caffeine, she would resume negotiations on the Hanlon house and score her client as many concessions as possible. She would schedule more house showings for next week. She would *not* think about how she should have been in Maui next week. On her honeymoon. As Mrs. Danica Malcom.

When Tate had called her last month to worm out of the wedding that had been scheduled for this Saturday, she'd canceled the week of vacation allotted for her honeymoon. But she'd left this weekend free. In retrospect, perhaps that had been a mistake. What was she planning to do on Saturday? Mope? Stare at the useless bridal gown in the back of her closet? Definitely not. Sulking wasn't her style.

So what if she was single? Dani kicked ass at her job. Focusing on that could help get her through the next few weeks, as well as boost her bank account. Some of the homes for sale in affluent Fulton county neighborhoods would bring very generous commissions.

As she entered the posh office building, the scent of coffee wafted down the corridor to meet her. She was still early enough that there wasn't yet a line stretching into the hall. The small coffee shop was wildly popular with those who worked in the twelve-story building. There was also a food court on the atrium level, but only one of the vendors opened for breakfast and the hot beverage options were limited.

She was just passing the elevator banks when her phone chirped, signaling a text. Had the owners of the two-story colonial in Dunwoody made a decision on her clients' offer? Without breaking stride, she pulled out the phone. The text was from Katie Whitman, Dani's passive-aggressive cousin who'd been furious that Dani hadn't asked her to be a bridesmaid.

I just heard!!! Like it wasn't bad enough he dumped u 3 wks before the wedding, now he's eloped? U poor thing. Ur better off w/out him. Total d-bag.

Dani growled involuntarily at the "poor thing." The d-bag assessment was accurate enough, but—

A muffled curse in a deep male voice cut through her preoccupation, followed by a pointed "excuse me."

Jerking her head up, Dani realized she'd nearly collided with a man exiting the coffee shop. And not just any man. She'd almost caused Hot Architect to dump his drink down the front of his expensive suit jacket. The dark-haired, broad-shouldered man—who was taller than her in spite of her heeled boots—worked for the design firm that took up the other half of the fifth floor, down the hall from the real-estate brokerage.

"I am so sorry." Shuffling back a step, she jammed the offending phone into her pocket. "I—"

"No harm done." His lips curved in an expression too fleeting to be deemed a true smile.

"But I feel—" *Like a dumbass klutz.* At one time, her father had been an Army Ranger instructor; Dani had been raised to be athletic and have quick reflexes. She'd helped get the Lady Vipers, her high-school basketball team, to the state championship. She was not clumsy. "I feel guilty," she concluded, trying to recall his name.

She'd overheard people calling him Mr. Grayson, but she wasn't sure about his first name. Ben? Bryan? The receptionist in Dani's office just called him Hot Architect. Since Dani had been engaged, she'd gone out of her way not to notice him or learn more about him.

Well, you're single now.

Very, very single. She was also close enough to appreciate his ice-blue eyes and the sexy contrast between his light gaze and thick hair even darker than hers, the last shade between brown and black. "Can I buy you a pastry to make up for it?" she offered impulsively.

He held up a small brown bag, indicating that he'd already fulfilled his pastry quota for the morning. "Maybe some other time." He spared another not-quite smile, then continued on his way, giving her a wide berth as he rounded the corner toward the elevators. Apparently, he wasn't drawn to women so busy snarling at their cell phones that they almost mowed down pedestrians. *Go figure.*

Then again, Dani was a goal-oriented person who welcomed challenges. Staring down the now-empty hall, she squared her shoulders. Coaxing a real smile from Mr. Grayson, one that actually reached those arresting eyes, had just made her to-do list.

BY LATE FRIDAY AFTERNOON, Dani had stopped second-guessing her decision not to work this weekend. *Self, I'm sorry I ever doubted you.* It would be for the good of all humanity if she avoided clients for a couple of days.

Normally, connecting buyers with a new house gave her warm fuzzy feelings. Growing up on assorted military bases, Dani used to wish for more stability, a true home. She liked to imagine her clients getting involved in their new communities, maybe raising families. But now, on the eve of her canceled wedding, she was finding it difficult not to gnash her teeth as she showed a redbrick three-bedroom to the Parkers, a pair of adorable newlyweds. They were currently debating whether to hang their wedding portrait in the foyer or over the mantel.

"The picture will look great anywhere," said the besotted husband. "How could it not when the bride in it is so beautiful?"

Dani managed not to roll her eyes. Sure, his petite auburn-haired wife was beautiful. But was that any guarantee he'd stay faithful?

When Tate had told Dani the international software company he worked for needed him in their Helsinki home office for four months, they'd made plans to visit each other and talk often. She'd gone to Finland once, after he'd had a few weeks to get settled, and he'd come to Atlanta for her birthday. The four-month assignment turned into six, though, and the time difference made phone conversations inconvenient. Still, Dani had seen plenty of military families overcome separation. She'd believed she and Tate could make the relationship work.

She certainly hadn't expected him to cheat on her. Dani had initiated sex more than he did. When he'd first gone overseas, she'd emailed him a provocative picture of herself. He'd asked her not to do it again. He'd claimed it reminded him of what he couldn't have, but she'd thought she detected a note of censure in his tone.

Well, he was out of her life now. Maybe she'd have a photographer take a picture of her scantily clad and hang that over *her* mantel.

Returning to the task at hand, she led Mr. and Mrs. Cute Couple to the recently remodeled kitchen, elaborating on the house's particulars. Two-car garage, plumbing on a septic system, great school district.

"Oh, we won't have to worry about school for years," the woman said dismissively. "We're in no hurry to have kids."

Her husband pulled her into his arms. "Agreed. I want you all to myself for a while." Bending down, he whispered something in her ear that caused a happy blush to steal across her face. Then he kissed her.

Hellooo—standing right here. But antagonizing clients was unwise for someone who worked on commission, so Dani kept her thoughts to herself. Giving the Parkers a moment of privacy, she meandered to the bay window and studied the pine trees and dogwoods dotting the generously sized yard.

Behind her, Mrs. Parker giggled. "We're going to

check out that master bedroom one more time, just for a second. I want another look at...the closet space."

Yeah.

"Feel free," Dani said with a tight smile. The previous inhabitants had already moved out, so at least she didn't have to worry about the frisky newlyweds hitting someone else's mattress. She figured they just wanted to steal a heated kiss or two.

Meanwhile, she tried not to feel bitter or envious; her neglected libido had been making itself known lately. She wasn't usually one for casual sex, but how was it fair that *she*—who'd been faithful to a fault—was going without while the cheating scumbag who'd replaced her with someone who "makes a man feel needed" was getting busy with his new bride? *Excuse the hell out of me for being able to open a pickle jar without assistance.*

When Tate originally called off the wedding, it had been difficult not to hope he met with some freak accident—like an anvil falling on his head. But she'd told herself to be adult about the situation. Wasn't it better that he ended things before the wedding instead of deciding afterward that they'd made a mistake? So instead of wishing him dead, she'd merely hoped that the next house he bought had termites and mold in the walls.

What she hadn't yet known was that getting dumped was only half the story. Earlier this week, he'd asked her to dinner. Since she had a box of his belongings to give back to him, she'd agreed. The diamond solitaire engagement ring was not among the returns. She'd hocked that to help cover nonrefundable wedding expenses she and her dad had incurred.

When Tate had broken up with her from the safe distance of Europe, he'd mentioned that "someone else" had helped him realize he didn't fully love his fiancée. But Dani hadn't expected that faceless someone to return to Georgia with him. As she'd learned during their strained dinner together, Tate and Ella had eloped last Saturday—exactly one week before he'd been scheduled to marry Dani.

"You deserved to hear it from me, in person, before we begin announcing it to family and friends." He'd adopted an expression of such condescending concern that she'd been tempted to punch him in the face. "I know this must be very hard on you."

"Not so much." She'd risen from her chair, abandoning a perfectly yummy shrimp carbonara. "Ella is welcome to you."

Truthfully, after six months of living on separate continents, Dani didn't miss him as much as she would have expected. She was almost as ticked off about the months of one-sided celibacy as she was about his defection. She'd always found serenity through physical outlets. Right now, frustrated and wanting to reclaim some feminine pride, she could really use a long night of sweaty, athletic—

"Danica? I think we're done inside the house." The lanky man and his auburn-haired bride had returned. "If you'll walk us through the yard and the garage, that should do it. Annette and I need some time alone to talk over everything we've seen today."

"Of course. Right this way." She opened the back door, leading them out onto a narrow deck. "The deck was added on, but the owners hired a professional to build it."

She often warned clients to be careful of homes full of DIY projects; not all of them held up well over time.

Sometimes, amateur wiring jobs went up in flames. Substandard roofing collapsed. Kind of like her love life.

THE CELL PHONE vibrated in the dashboard cup holder. Dani groaned. Another pitying relative or acquaintance? But then she glimpsed the picture of her best friend, Meg Rafferty, on the screen. Under different circumstances, both women would have been en route to the famous Swan House right now for a rehearsal dinner. Afterward, there was supposed to have been a bachelorette party hosted in the lingerie store Meg co-owned.

Using the phone's earpiece, Dani answered. "Hello."

"It's officially after five o'clock," Meg said. "A socially accepted time for booze. Want to meet somewhere for drinks?"

It was a Friday night. If they went out, would they be surrounded by couples on dates? Showing that last house to the Parkers had been all the exposure to couples Dani could stand. A girls' night in was a possibility, but Meg had recently moved in with her current boyfriend. *Which leaves my place.* When her last lease ran out and she hadn't been able to negotiate anything shorter than six months, she'd moved into a tiny, unimpressive apartment. She wasn't supposed to have been there this long. The plan had been for her and Tate to house hunt when he returned from Europe. Meg knew how much Dani disliked the "temporary" apartment. Every time she came over, she vacillated between sympathy and outrage on her friend's behalf.

"Thanks for the offer," Dani said, "but I'm way behind on paperwork. I want to use the free evening to catch up." *Liar.* She sighed. "Actually, what I really want is to get laid."

There was a startled pause, followed by a snicker. "I can't help you there."

"Don't worry. You aren't who I had in mind."

"Wait, there's someone specific? Why have I not heard about him?"

"No, no one specific. I just meant…" Yet she couldn't help envisioning Hot Architect. This morning, they'd passed again in the hall and she'd made a comically exaggerated show of watching where she was going so as not to bump anyone. Amusement had twinkled in his pale blue eyes, and his lips had twitched. She'd *almost* rated a grin.

"Sorry, I didn't catch the end of that sentence. Did you lose your train of thought or are you going through a tunnel? *Or,*" Meg added knowingly, "did you suddenly remember that you suck at lying? Out with it! Who is this mystery man who has you hot and bothered?"

"You remember that time you picked me up at the office for lunch and Judy was rhapsodizing about the architect who works down the hall?"

"Bryce Grayson?"

Dani smacked her hand against the steering wheel. "Bryce, yes! I knew it started with a *B*. Thank you."

"I've caught glimpses of him." Meg gave a low whistle. "Nice. I mean, I only have eyes for Nolan, of course, but…*damn*."

"Exactly. I worked hard not to notice him while I was with Tate, but now I am a free woman." A free woman with a healthy sex drive.

Bryce was going to smile at her soon, and the natural next step would be conversation. With any luck, they wouldn't stop there.

2

SEAN GRAYSON WINKED conspiratorially at the perky woman in yoga pants. Between the cartoon character on her T-shirt and her braided pigtails, she looked more like a teenager than his twin brother's secretary. "I really appreciate your taking time out of your Saturday to let me in."

She shrugged. "This is on my way to the gym. Just promise to lock up when you leave or Bryce will have my head on a platter. I'd better scoot, or I'll be late for Zumba." Pausing in the doorway, she asked over her shoulder, "You know what would be hilarious? If Bryce had the same idea and *he's* secretly at *your* office right now, setting up a surprise for Monday."

Bitterness stabbed at Sean, an unpleasant sensation somewhere between loss and anger. Alone in the spacious offices of Bertram Design Associates, he tried to imagine stepping into the trailer on his current job site and finding it filled with balloons and streamers. *Never in a million years.* He and Bryce might be identical twins, but these days, they had little in common besides looks and a shared birthday.

Bryce, older by nine minutes, had always been more studious, diligently making A-honor roll and graduating high school as valedictorian. Sean had excelled in different areas, like industrial arts and varsity football... and making time with the varsity cheerleaders. Despite different interests, the two brothers had encouraged each other. They'd been close. Then Bryce had been awarded a major scholarship to a college out of state.

Sean stayed behind, working for their dad's roofing company and pooling his money with his parents' to afford a trade school degree, eventually working his way up to supervising construction crews. When their dad suffered a heart attack—minor, but alarming—Bryce had been too busy with finals to come home. There were holiday breaks and summers when Bryce chose plans with his frat brothers or staying on campus for intern opportunities over visiting his family. After graduation, he'd returned to Georgia, but he'd been different. He was more polished and educated than anyone else in the family, and he never let Sean forget it.

Most of the time, Sean told himself it was natural for siblings to grow apart, no big deal. But his last girlfriend had accused him of being jealous of his successful, intelligent brother. *"He has the prestigious degree, the loft condo and the class. You're a glorified handyman. No wonder you resent him."*

Was Sean here in part to prove her wrong? To try to recapture some of the old camaraderie? *Knock off the introspective crap. You're here to hang some balloons and heckle him about being old.*

It was only fair, considering how often Bryce had lorded his nine-minute head start on life over his "little brother" when they were kids. Sean also had a gift to leave on his brother's desk. He'd scanned a section of one of Bryce's first blueprints and paid a friend with graphics art talent to turn it into a one-of-a-kind multicolored kaleidoscope print. Sean had framed the resulting artwork and wrapped it in black "over the hill" paper. He hoped Bryce would hang the print in his office.

Or was the customized art too funky for the uptight man Bryce had become? Although Bryce was a decent architect, his main role in the company was getting permits passed. He was the person who crossed the t's and dotted the i's. As if his occupational habits were taking over his personal life, with each passing year, Bryce grew more rigid. His DVD collection of pretentious, independent films was probably alphabetized. Most of Sean's DVDs weren't even in their proper cases.

Unlike his brother, Sean lived in the moment, enjoying spontaneity. Why overplan the journey? In his experience, life offered many interesting detours.

OF ALL THE ways Dani could have spent Saturday afternoon, hiding in an empty office so that concerned friends couldn't call her home line or drop by to check on her was definitely in the pathetic top five.

Granted, she'd spent the past few hours putting herself in a strategic position to reach her goal—the youngest top seller to graduate to a flat desk fee instead of splitting commission with the brokerage—but was it really healthy to be so practical? She was a scorned bride. Shouldn't she be finding catharsis in some kind of outrageous behavior? In her career, following the rules and setting goals worked well. In her love life?

Not so much. *Tate* was the one who'd cheated, yet he was happily married while she was alone.

When Meg had announced she was moving in with Nolan, a pharmaceutical sales rep six years her senior, after dating him only a couple of months, Dani had cautioned her exuberant friend that it was too soon. But Meg had defied conventional wisdom and seemed perfectly happy with her choice. Meanwhile, Dani had tried to do everything right with Tate—spending a year and a half getting to know him before they got engaged, being completely supportive of his needing to work out of the country—and she'd gotten screwed.

If this were a movie, she would have taken her canceled honeymoon to Maui all by herself and fallen in love with one of Hollywood's leading men amid a learning-to-surf montage and funny luau scene. *Well, it's not a movie.* So she could either stay here and continue her downward spiral into feeling sorry for herself or she could call Meg. Maybe last night's invitation for drinks still stood. Or maybe Dani should look around the area for paintball places with evening hours. She sort of liked the idea of wearing her pristine white wedding dress to a paintball battle. If nothing else, the sight would unnerve her opponents.

She heaved a sigh. It wasn't the bridal gown's fault that Tate was too insecure to spend his life with a strong woman. She shouldn't take out her rage on a seven-hundred-dollar dress. But she could totally take it out on a pitcher's worth of margaritas.

Resolved, she shut down her computer. There was *one* nice thing about her abysmal little apartment; it was only two adjoining parking lots away from a neighborhood bar. She could easily walk home after a few drinks. The bar was a nice place with pool tables and a Saturday happy hour she might still make if she left now. Maybe Meg could meet her there.

Dani would call her from the car, once her cell phone was plugged in to the charger. She'd "accidentally" forgotten to charge it this morning. At least, that was the story she planned to give anyone who'd been unable to reach her. Her father had called three times alone that morning. Lord knew how many voice messages awaited her.

When Dani had arrived at the office, she'd been wearing a three-quarter sleeved semitransparent blouse over a lace-edged red camisole and white denim skirt. But the air-conditioning didn't run on the weekends and the day had turned into one of those humid summer previews when Mother Nature demonstrated what Atlanta had to look forward to in June, so she'd shrugged out of the blouse. Now she scooped up the discarded garment and her briefcase, suddenly eager to escape the barren office and the loneliness it represented. She could imagine how Tate would gloat if he knew she'd spent the day here alone.

But it turned out the building wasn't entirely deserted. As she juggled her belongings in her arms to lock the brokerage door, she heard footsteps in the hall behind her. She glanced back immediately; her dad, who'd been far more comfortable teaching her self-defense than taking her bra shopping, had coached her to be aware of her surroundings.

Her eyes widened. Hot Architect! It was like a sign. Or fate, if she believed in such nonsense. *For today, be a believer.* "Hi."

"Hi," he echoed. "I didn't think anyone else was

cooped up in the building on such a gorgeous day." His lips quirked in a lazy half smile, his gaze dropping in a brief but appreciative once-over before returning to meet hers. "Never been so happy to be wrong."

He was *flirting* with her? His unexpectedly playful tone was like diving into cold water on a scorching summer day—an initial shock to the system, but damn it felt good.

Although he still hadn't given her a full smile, humor danced in his eyes. "I hope your presence here on a Saturday afternoon doesn't mean you're a stuffy workaholic," he teased. "That would be tragic. But I'm willing to give you the benefit of the doubt."

"You're here, too. Workaholic tendencies?"

She could almost believe the man she normally saw in well-tailored suits was a workaholic. But now? *Lord have mercy.* His dark hair was rumpled. With no trace of styling product, it looked shaggier yet sexy. He filled out a pair of jeans in a way that could make a grown woman weep, and his T-shirt… She tried not to gape, scarcely believing how he'd hid those biceps under his suit jackets.

He crossed his arms over his chest, giving her a great view of corded forearms. "I wouldn't describe myself as a workaholic." This time, instead of the half smile, he flashed a wicked grin. "But I don't stop until the job's done to everyone's mutual satisfaction."

Her mind raced, full of suggestions on how such satisfaction could be reached. Hadn't she promised herself that when he finally smiled at her, she'd make a move?

"Are you on your way to the elevators?" he asked.

"Stairwell, actually. I prefer physical activity."

His grin widened. There was a bracketed indentation to the right of his mouth, not deep enough or boy-ish enough to be called a dimple, but close. "Sounds like you and I have a lot in common."

Two days ago, she'd offered the innocuous sugges-tion of buying him a pastry. Now she wanted to offer a whole lot more than that. Dinner, maybe. And des-sert, back at her place. *Slow your roll, Yates. The guy doesn't even know your name yet.* "I'm Danica, by the way. My friends call me Dani."

"Mine call me Grayson. Or just Gray." He reached out to shake her hand, his fingers calloused and warm against her skin. She suddenly wanted to know what that touch would feel like along the rest of her body.

"Do you have anywhere you have to be?" She blurted the question before she could change her mind. "Be-cause, personally, I'm dying to let off some steam."

Heat flared in his eyes, his smile fading into some-thing more intense. "What did you have in mind?"

"For starters, a drink at a bar I know." The delicious way he was looking at her made her reckless and light-headed. "After that…well, I guess we'll see."

He stepped closer. They weren't touching, but the proximity was intimate. Her body prickled in height-ened awareness and if her hands weren't full, she'd be fanning herself. "Consider my evening cleared."

Wow. She was really doing this. Exhilaration and desire were a potent mix, an electric buzz along her nerves.

They fell in step together, and he opened the door for her when they reached the stairwell. Dani walked up and down these same concrete steps on a daily basis, but it had never felt thrilling or sexy before. Gray's pres-ence heightened her senses, made her more aware of her own body. As she descended the stairs in front of him, she swore she could *feel* his admiring gaze drop to her hips and butt. The ogling wasn't unwanted. After all, she was the one who'd propositioned him. And holding the attention of such an incredibly sexy man made her feel powerful and feminine. Boldly sensual.

While she'd never been shy, even she was surprised at how brazenly she was behaving. She'd daydreamed about making a move on him when he finally smiled at her, but she'd had no idea how hot the chemistry would be between them. It made her wild impulse to take him home feel inevitable rather than insane.

Still, one-night stands were uncharted territory for her. At this precise moment, tasting his kisses seemed like the best idea she'd ever had, but would she feel that way the next time they ran into each other outside the coffee place? What would it be like to stand in line for a latte behind a guy who'd seen her naked?

As they reached the exit, she took a deep breath. "No matter what happens tonight, you don't have to worry that seeing me will be awkward when Monday rolls around or that I'll crowd you."

"Monday?" he echoed. Evidently, he hadn't thought that far ahead yet.

She gave him an earnest look over her shoulder, wanting to clarify that there were no strings. "I'm definitely not looking for a relationship. I was supposed to get married in…" She consulted the slim gold watch around her wrist. "Forty-five minutes. My fiancé eloped last weekend with the woman he was seeing on the side. Right now, I need to have a really good time and forget the whole mess." Permanently, if possible.

Did her words make it sound as if she'd picked him

at random? "I've been thinking about you all week," she added. "And it seems like the attraction's mutual. What do you say, Bryce?"

He frowned.

"Gray," she corrected. He'd said the nickname was what his friends used, and she was hoping they would become very friendly before the night was over. "Want to help generate a little amnesia?"

3

IDIOT, IDIOT, IDIOT. Sean wanted to howl at the bitter unfairness of the situation, at his own stupidity. He was in his brother's office building, so why the hell hadn't it occurred to him that the stunning brunette had mistaken him for Bryce? Maybe because no one had confused the two of them since second grade. They were too dissimilar.

The disappointment at hearing his twin's name from Dani's full, cupid's bow lips stabbed deep. The idea of his brother flirting with her, touching her... His hands clenched into fists at his sides. Then again, she must not know Bryce, or why would she have introduced herself? Sean spared a moment of contemptuous disbelief for his permit-seeking, suit-wearing brother. The man worked down the hall from a woman who looked like this and had never even asked her *name*?

Idiocy must run in the family.

As he mentally berated both himself and his brother, Dani's forehead crinkled. "Damn," she sighed, regret lacing her husky voice. Had she taken his silence as rejection? "Was I too forward?"

"What? No. Actually, I like that in a woman." A lot. She was gorgeous, with her wild fall of dark hair and her long, lean body, but what made her sexy as hell was the sense that she knew what she wanted and wasn't shy about going after it. When she'd first seen him in the hallway, the awareness in her gaze had been like a wave of heat, burning a tantalizing path.

He'd always been drawn to brunettes. In her body-hugging top, nails painted a fearless red, she looked like his fantasy made real. But, odds were, when he told her he wasn't Bryce, she was going to be mortified.

They'd reached the parking lot. When he informed her of her mistake, would she bolt for her car? She'd be gone from his life as suddenly as she'd appeared. Everything inside him protested at the idea.

Guilt warred with lust. Sean was ready and willing to help her forget her problems and bolster her wounded ego. *But she wants Bryce.* Except, Bryce wouldn't have been any good to her. Mr. Rules and Regulations would never go home with a woman whose name he'd only just learned; he'd be appalled by the very idea. If Dani wanted a good time, then she had—however inadvertently—chosen the right brother.

Even Sean's ex-girlfriend, the one who'd despaired of his never amounting to anything, had said so. Tara's parting words echoed in his mind. *"If you and that sophisticated twin of yours could be combined into one person, you'd be the perfect guy. He's the one with ambition and smarts...but, let's face it, you sure know how to show a girl a good time."*

Unaware of his mental anguish, Dani smiled. "As long as I'm being blunt and inappropriate anyway, can I just say, now that I've seen you in short sleeves, I think it's a shame you wear all those jackets?" Her gaze went to his arm, as tangible and arousing as a caress. She was attracted to *him*. Specifically.

It was impossible not to return her grin. "Want me to flex or anything? I live to serve."

"Then have that drink with me," she coaxed.

He took an involuntary step closer, breathing in her honey and vanilla scent. How could any man refuse her? "Absolutely."

I CAN'T BELIEVE I'm doing this! Dani's gaze darted to the rearview mirror, as if she had to make sure Gray's SUV was still there. Without the physical evidence, this seemed more like a naughty daydream than real life. Her skin was tingling all over. Between adrenaline and hormones, she had to squeeze her fingers around the steering wheel to keep them from trembling.

Back in the parking lot, before they'd gone to their own cars, she'd thought he might kiss her. She'd barely been able to tear her gaze from his mouth. Had he been able to tell how hard her pulse was pounding? She'd been so turned-on that anything they'd done would have felt natural. The drive to the bar, however, allowed just enough time for nerves to creep in.

It had been months since she'd had sex and years since she'd been with anyone other than her ex-fiancé. Needing moral support, she instructed her phone to call Meg.

"Hey," her friend answered, sounding relieved. "I'm glad it's you! I've been trying to give you space today, in case you didn't feel like talking, but—"

"I don't mean to cut you off, but we don't have much time."

"Well, that sounds dramatic. Like, you're fleeing the country from bad guys and need to tell me you've left something important in a bus-station locker. Or you're going to ask me whether you should cut the blue wire or the red wire."

Dani laughed. Apparently, all the action movies she made her friend watch had left an impression. "I went into the office today, and Hot Architect was there! Well, Gray." In the military, nicknames were common; she rarely thought anything of using them. But calling him Gray felt intimate and gave her a rush of pleasure. "Short for his last name, Grayson."

"You're already on a nickname basis?" Meg asked, sounding impressed. "You work fast."

You don't know the half of it. "I have to tell you something, and if you love me, you won't talk me out of this."

"This promises to be good," Meg said cheerfully. "And I think we both know I'm the 'jump out of the plane, worry about the parachute on the way down' friend. *You're* the voice of reason who talks *me* out of things. Or tries to—I rarely listen to good sense."

Maybe Meg's "seize the day" attitude is rubbing off on me. "Gray's in the car behind me right now, following me to the bar in front of my complex. And if things go well over drinks…"

Meg let out a squeal of delight. "You're taking him home with you!"

"I haven't decided for sure." *The hell you haven't,* her libido argued. "Would sleeping with him be completely crazy?" Not that sane had gotten her anywhere, except dumped and relocated to a crappy apartment.

"Crazy's what you need tonight. Celebrate your freedom! Instead of tying the knot, you can tie up Hot Architect."

Dani grinned. "So much for any worry that you might judge me for seducing a stranger." Despite how often their paths crossed, she knew almost nothing about him.

"No judging! But for safety's sake, check in with me tonight and again in the morning. If I don't get proof of life, I'm showing up at your place with Nolan."

Morning? Recalling how good Gray looked in his black T-shirt, she shivered. What would it be like to wake up in those muscular arms? Assuming he was the kind of guy who stayed the night instead of leaving afterward.

"I'm not getting up early just so I can run out for a paper with the date on it and send you a picture," Dani joked, "but I will text you." She was grateful to have someone who looked out for her. The two of them had met in the waiting area of a salon four years ago, striking up conversation over the trials of curly hair in a humid climate, and now they were as close as sisters. Meg had even tried to fix up Dani with one of her brothers, saying that if things worked out they could be sisters-in-law.

"I'm keeping my phone by me for the rest of the night," Meg said. "And hoping for salacious details."

Dani braked at a red light, swallowing hard. The bar was on the left just on the other side of the intersection. "I'm about to turn into the parking lot."

"Okay. All kidding aside, there's something you should consider. As your best friend, I have to ask…are you wearing good first-impression underwear? Please tell me it's something from the store!" Meg extended Dani a special friends-and-family discount.

Dani laughed, her nerves dissipating. "Sorry to disappoint you, but I'm wearing plain cotton. The set matches. Do I at least get credit for that?"

Would Gray have preferred something lacy and silk to the basic sky-blue pieces? Then again, depending on how the evening went, maybe she wouldn't be wearing them for long.

DANI CONGRATULATED HERSELF on fitting the car into such a narrow parking space—it was admirable that she'd done a precision job considering her shaky hands and accelerated pulse. She figured the adrenaline in her system was one part nerves, two parts sheer sexual anticipation. By the time she'd taken a deep breath and gathered her purse, Gray had reached her driver-side door.

He opened the door for her and extended his hand to help her out of the car. Old-fashioned gallantry, or was he simply as eager to touch her as she was him? His fingers grazed her palm, which she'd never considered a sensitive part of her body before today. Now, sensation shivered through her.

"Thanks," she said, hearing the slight, breathless catch in her voice.

"It seemed like the chivalrous thing to do." Though his expression remained deadpan, wicked humor glinted in his eyes. "Wouldn't want you to think you were out with less than a perfect gentleman."

"Honestly? I'd rather spend tonight with an imperfect one."

That earned her a low, rich laugh. "Then you definitely have the right guy."

As she preceded him inside, it took a moment for her eyes to adjust to the dim interior. The bar had a cool, cave-like feel, with few windows overlooking the parking lot and street. But it was a classy cave—no smoke or scarred tables—boasting a quality list of domestic and imported beers.

Gray looked around. "Private booth, or would you rather sit at the bar?"

As nice as the private part sounded, she felt too restless to sit. Being this close to him had her buzzing with energy. "Third option—pool table. Do you play?"

"Yeah." He smiled sheepishly. "But I should warn you, I can get pretty competitive."

Something else they had in common. "That's okay. My friend Meg says I redefine the word." Dani had taken a game night with the Raffertys a little too seriously last summer, and Meg's family still teased her about it. But Major Yates had raised his daughter to be goal oriented. Sportsmanship had been more of an afterthought.

Gray smirked. "Then this should be interesting."

At the bar, they asked about table availability and got a set of balls. Cues and racks hung by the tables. The cashier assured them a waitress frequently circulated the pool area and would take their drink orders soon. To the right of the main seating area, a short set of stairs led down to a recessed pool hall. The row of six pool tables was separated from the rest of the bar with a railed half wall. The opposite wall was completely mirrored, reflecting a rainbow of neon from various beer signs.

Two of the tables were still vacant, and Dani went

immediately to the one farthest from other players. A drink menu sat on the railing between a couple of leather-topped stools. Gray picked it up, flipping through the laminated pages.

"You want a look at this?" he asked.

She shook her head, gaze locked on his. "Not necessary. I know exactly what I want."

Being cheated on was tough on a girl's self-esteem. But with one steamy glance, Gray managed to restore any confidence she'd lost over the past month. For a second, he looked dazed, and it was heady, having an effect on a man so ridiculously sexy.

He recovered quickly. "Well, don't be shy. Let's hear it."

You. On that pool table. "Draft beer."

"So you don't go for the froufrou drinks?" He tilted his chin toward a waitress at the far end of the pool hall. On her tray were two foamy drinks in varying shades of pink and something bright blue in a glass the size of a small fishbowl, complete with a swizzle stick of impaled fruit.

"Drinks with paper umbrellas have their place," Dani said. "Like, if I'm poolside at some tropical resort. Champagne—*expensive* champagne—is for when I close on a high-dollar property, tequila shots are for bad breakups, sangria is for TV show marathons with my best friend. But draft beer is for when I'm about to kick some guy's ass in eight ball."

"Then maybe you should be more concerned about the right drink for when you fall a dismal second."

She grinned, liking the pure challenge in his voice. "I don't know what beverage that could be. You'll have to tell me after you lose."

The waitress reached them a few seconds later. Dani ordered a Belgian white they had on tap. Gray asked for a dark ale. As the waitress departed, the two of them selected cue sticks and continued quizzing each other on the right cocktails for increasingly absurd occasions.

"When your team wins the Super Bowl?" Gray asked.

"Alabama slammer. What about if you win an Academy Award?"

"Famous gold statue? Goldschläger, obviously. Toasting your fortieth birthday?"

"Something sophisticated and grown-up. A martini, maybe?" She shrugged. "I'm nowhere close to knowing that one."

"Me, neither. Monday's my thirty-fourth birthday."

"Oh." His birthday was in two days? "Happy birthday."

He gave her a wolfish smile. "As early celebrations go, today has been off the charts."

Did he see her as his gift to himself? She swallowed, hoping she lived up to his expectations. "Perfect cocktail for a zombie apocalypse?"

"Rookie mistake. Zombie apocalypse is the time to stay sober. It's critical to keep a clear head and steady shooting hand for those all-important double taps."

She laughed. "Good point."

After the waitress returned with their drinks, Gray clarified that they were playing basic eight ball and that they had to call their intended shots.

"Hell, yes," Dani insisted. "Miss your pocket, lose your turn."

He set the plastic triangle on the green felt. "Ladies first?"

"Or we could lag for the break," she said, suggesting the more official method of shooting a ball off the far rail. Whoever's ball came back closest would break.

"Serious player," he said approvingly. "Most of my construction buddies just flip a coin."

Construction buddies? Dani knew it wasn't uncommon for architects to visit build sites, so it shouldn't surprise her that he had friends among the construction crews. Yet she had trouble picturing the man who normally wore expensive suits, the one who was so reserved he'd never fully smiled at her until today, trash-talking construction guys over beer and pool. She started to tell him that he seemed different, which she meant as a compliment, but she couldn't think of a way to say it that wouldn't make him sound previously aloof or stuffy. Weren't most people more likely to loosen up on the weekends? *So stop overanalyzing and just be thankful you ran into him on a Saturday.*

They each selected a solid-colored ball and shot for the foot rail. The balls rolled back, hers stopping a fraction of an inch before his.

"Your break," she said.

"Close, though." He gave her a look of mock regret. "I guess a player with your skill isn't likely to do the girl thing, huh?"

"Girl thing?"

He sipped his beer. "You know, where you ask a big strong guy to help you with your form so he has a reason to put his arms around you."

Dani stepped forward, leaning her pool cue against the railing. Looking intrigued, he set down his beer as she moved closer, invading his personal space.

She reached for his hand. His fingers were cool from

the beer, but heat rolled through her anyway. "I'm a woman, not a girl. If I want a man to touch me, I don't need a lame excuse." She settled his hand on the curve of her hip, her pulse kicking up a notch when they were close enough that they could have been kissing.

His eyes were mesmerizing, light-colored but blazing with intensity. "Good to know." Raising his free hand, he traced her lower lip with the pad of his thumb. Desire had been sparking inside her since the moment he'd smiled at her in the office hallway, but now a pang of sharp arousal jolted her—and they were fully dressed in a public place. Imagining the kind of magic he could work in the privacy of her apartment left her dizzy.

If she didn't move away from him, she would be in no condition to shoot pool accurately. Which might not matter in the larger scheme of things, but she had to admit, part of her wanted to impress him.

When she stepped back, reaching for her drink, Gray gave her one more scorching look, then took his place at the table. The competitor in her wanted to watch the balls scatter and check for strategic positioning; the female in her was having difficulty looking away from the back of his jeans. When he'd said earlier that he liked physical activity, it had obviously been more than innuendo. He was in fantastic shape.

"You're up," he said, drawing her attention back to the game.

She scanned the table. He'd pocketed the seven, so she was stripes. She called the eleven and leaned down to take her shot. Recalling the appreciative way she'd watched *him* shoot, she stole an involuntary glance toward the mirrored wall at the last second. His reflected gaze locked on hers—avid and hungry—and she fumbled her shot. The eleven rolled in right where it was supposed to, but the cue ball followed.

Annoyed with herself for the undisciplined lapse in concentration, she let loose a stream of profanity.

Behind her, Gray laughed. "You kiss your mother with that mouth?"

"Actually, she died when I was a baby."

He paled. "Oh, God. I'm—"

"You didn't know." Whenever she told someone about her mom, she felt as if she should be sadder, but she didn't remember the woman at all. The deepest sorrow she'd experienced was for her father's loss. "My dad raised me and, incidentally, taught me most of the bad words I know. He wasn't above swearing at soldiers if it motivated them, and sometimes he forgot to turn it off at home."

"Military, huh?"

She nodded. "Army."

"My father had his own roofing company and took on a lot of small construction jobs for extra income. He was careful, but anyone who works with tools that often is gonna catch his thumb with a hammer from time to time or run afoul of a circular saw." He smiled. "Colorful words abounded. Of course, he swore me to secrecy. Mom would've had a fit if she'd known the vocabulary I was picking up in the garage."

He surveyed the table, nostalgia fading as he immersed himself in the game. Using the conveniently positioned stripes, he knocked in two easy shots before having to stop and think about what he wanted to do next.

"If I were a show-off," he said, "this is where I'd impress you with some fancy trick shot."

She smirked over the rim of her beer. "In my experience, guys who really know how to handle their sticks don't need to compensate with trick moves."

"Need? No. But nothing wrong with spicing things up every now and then, right?" Giving her a suggestive smile, he executed a perfect behind-the-back shot.

She bit back her own smile. "I refuse to contribute to your ego by applauding that."

"You can admit I make you weak in the knees. I won't lose respect for you."

She snorted. He sank a fourth ball before finally missing. Dani used the opportunity to reclaim her dignity with a great stop shot. The waitress brought another round of drinks while Dani pocketed two more, steadily closing the gap. But then she was left without a shot. Even as she banked the cue ball as best she could, she held no real hope. Sometimes, physics was against you.

Gray returned to the table. She sipped her beer, watching in admiration as he ran the table. His cockiness at pool was well warranted. After knocking in the eight ball for the win, he sauntered back to the railing with a satisfied smile.

"Now I wish we'd bet something," he said. "Or that I'd suggested strip pool."

The idea was appealing, if either of them had a pool table at home. She slid off her stool and began gathering the balls to rerack. "You can't play strip pool in public."

He joined her at the table, leaning close as he lowered his voice. "Sure you can." His breath feathered against her ear, a tantalizing tickle of warmth. "You just have to remove things that aren't obvious to everyone else in the room." For the second time that night, he cupped her hip. Then he traced a finger across the denim, just above the elastic band of her panties. "Like…earrings."

His outrageous teasing made her laugh, and she shoved against his chest. "You are a bad man."

He dipped his head in agreement. "Being bad is my best quality."

4

"Nice job." It was damned uncommon for Sean Grayson to smile when he lost, but he couldn't help an admiring grin as Dani pocketed the winning ball in their second game.

She was a worthy opponent. Plus, she was sexy as hell. Watching her lean over in that narrow skirt that hinted at naughtiness without actually revealing anything lessened the sting of defeat. "Best two out of three?" It was a logical suggestion, given that they were currently tied and that the waitress had just brought them a basket of chips and salsa to go with another round of beers. Yet, the longer he spent here with Dani, the more desperate he was to get her alone.

The heated glances they'd shared had escalated to casual—and not so casual—touches. He wanted her. Badly. If his jeans grew any tighter, he wasn't sure he'd be able to keep playing.

"One more," she agreed. Her dark eyes gleamed with pleasure. Because she was having such a good time? Or because, like him, she was looking forward to what would follow their next match? She'd made it clear with her flirtatious words and body language that she desired him every bit as much as he desired her. "I hate to end on ties."

He chuckled. "Right? There should always be a clear winner. My mom used to get aggravated at me and my brother for being too compet—" He stopped abruptly. With Dani calling him Gray, like most of his buddies did, and that way she had of grinning up at him as if he were the only man in the world who mattered, he'd almost managed to forget that she thought he was someone else.

"Lost my train of thought," he mumbled.

She nodded absently, her easy acceptance of his fib making him feel like scum. As far as she knew, she had no reason to mistrust him. "You go ahead and rack 'em," she suggested. "I'm going to run to the ladies' room."

Five minutes ago, he would have watched her cross the pool hall, enjoying the view and the graceful, confident way she moved. Now, he was preoccupied with guilt. His almost-mention of Bryce had taken some of the shine off the evening.

A beautiful woman who was supposed to be at her own wedding reception right now had entreated him to show her a good time and help her forget a broken engagement. When he'd agreed, he hadn't been thinking any further than this evening. But now, thoughts of his brother brought unwelcome reality with them. Unless he swung by Bryce's house tomorrow and somehow convinced his twin to quit his job and never step foot in his office again, odds were, Dani would run into him at some point. Even though she'd stipulated that she only wanted someone for tonight, that she wouldn't cling or act differently afterward, Sean couldn't let her face someone she mistakenly believed she'd been intimate with.

Sean could give her exactly what she wanted—a raw, passionate night with a near stranger to keep her mind off the wedding that hadn't happened. But before he left, he'd have to find a way to tell her the truth. *In which case, she'll probably never speak to you again.*

The realization sucked. He'd known within moments of meeting Dani that he was attracted to her, but over the past couple of hours, he'd discovered he really liked her. She was smart and sassy, shot excellent pool, didn't seem to have a pretentious bone in her body and, when provoked, had the R-rated vocabulary of a cranky trucker. She was all wrong for Bryce, but exactly the kind of woman Sean could picture himself falling for—except he wouldn't have the chance to fall. They only had tonight.

Which was what she'd wanted in the first place, he reminded himself. She wasn't ready to consider relationships or dating. She'd been very clear about her request—a single, reckless night. And if that was all he got, he planned to make it count.

BY WINNING THE second game, Dani had put herself back in the running for overall victory. In theory, she was good enough to win their final match, too. Yet she was having a hell of a time trying to focus. Ever since she'd returned from the ladies' room, it seemed as if the sexual tension between her and Gray had grown even more electric, crackling all around them with its own magnetic pull. He was as wickedly charming as he'd been all night, but there was no more playfulness in his expression.

Now, the way he watched her bordered on predatory. He was biding his time but would eventually pounce. And she couldn't wait.

She swallowed, her throat dry with anticipation. She flagged down the waitress and requested a glass of ice water. Though she was hardly impaired, three beers had softened the edges of the world. She knew what was going to happen after this final game, and she wanted to be able to participate fully, alert enough to register every delicious detail. When morning came, she didn't want her memories of the night to be vague or hazy. Especially not if Gray was as good in bed as she expected.

Lost in prurient thoughts, she miscued her shot. She was still muttering curse words when he joined her, tugging gently at one of her curls.

"You have quite a mouth," he drawled.

"That a complaint?" she asked, knowing from his expression it wasn't.

"Yes." His gaze slid to her lips. "Because your mouth has been distracting the hell out of me all night. I'm too busy imagining kissing you to think straight."

Same here. Except, her imagination hadn't exactly stopped with kissing.

Despite her innate competitive streak, right now, she couldn't bring herself to care about pool. She wanted Gray's mouth on her, his hands on her. Since she couldn't seem to find her voice, she met his eyes.

When he cupped her face with his hands, she experienced a giddy rush of excitement. Even though it had only been hours since they'd encountered each other at the office, it felt as if she'd been waiting forever for him to kiss her. His mouth settled over hers, and she parted her lips in invitation. She buried her fingers in his hair, surprised at how silky it was. Their kiss was salty and spicy, and her body pulsed with sensation.

Gray kissed the same way he shot pool, with bold assurance and innate skill. He speared his tongue into her mouth, his possessiveness nearly making her moan, then pulled back, teasing, nipping at her lower lip. She was glad she was balanced between him and the pool table. Despite mocking his earlier boast that he made her knees weak, the longer he kissed her, the less steady she felt.

His hands dropped to her hips, and he pulled her tightly against him. The hard length of his erection was unmistakable. An answering need pooled between her thighs. As much as she was enjoying their kiss, suddenly, it wasn't enough. The sensual hunger blooming inside her had turned ravening.

He must have felt the same way. Lifting his head, he reached for the eight ball on the table and swiped it into a pocket. "Oops." His breathing was rapid, his voice strained. "Guess I lose. Ready to get out of here?"

Wordlessly, she nodded. If she were any more ready, they'd be arrested for public indecency. A hundred detailed fantasies were bursting to life in her mind, but they all required the same starting point—getting this man alone. Immediately.

IRONICALLY, DESPITE DANI'S urgency to reach the seclusion of her apartment, the walk across the adjacent parking lots was taking twice as long as usual. Probably because she and Gray couldn't keep their hands off each other.

The starlit line of trees around the perimeter of her complex offered far more privacy than a pool hall. Gray spun her into his arms, taking her mouth in another kiss that made every nerve ending in her body sing with pleasure. But the pleasure was edged with rising desperation. Her breasts ached to be freed from their confines, bared to his touch. The humid spring night around them was silky against her skin, so soft it was a tease. She needed his calloused fingers on her, needed friction.

She moaned into the kiss, dimly aware that she was rubbing her body against his. "My place." She tugged his lip between her teeth. "I want you, but not so badly that I'm willing to embarrass myself in a parking lot." Only half sure she spoke the truth, she quickened her pace.

With his long legs, he easily matched her stride. "Dare I ask what you *are* willing to do?"

She could hear the smile in his voice, knew he was kidding, but that didn't stop her fevered mind from creating vivid images in silent reply. "Keep up and you'll find out."

It wasn't until she turned her key in the lock that she experienced a tiny splinter of shyness. Beyond the physical intimacy of what they were about to do, there was a certain amount of intimacy in simply bringing him home. She'd leased the place a few months ago, when she was still engaged, and had never had a man here.

As if sensing a change in her mood, Gray massaged her neck soothingly, circling his thumb at her nape, applying just the right amount of heavenly pressure. "Everything okay?"

"Yeah." Resolutely, she opened the door. "I was just thinking I should warn you, I'm not the world's most diligent housekeeper."

She flipped on the lamp that sat on a small entry table along with her mail. It didn't offer much illumination, only a minimal rebuff against the darkness beyond. Still, it was enough that he'd be able to notice her habit of haphazardly kicking off her shoes when she walked through the door. Open-toed pumps and platform wedges were scattered about, some fallen on their sides like defeated warriors in a mythical shoe battle. Since she hadn't expected to return from the office with a date, she hadn't bothered to tidy the client files, property brochures and books on real estate that cluttered her living room.

"I mean, I'm not a slob," she defended herself. She never left the apartment with dirty dishes out, and she'd put fresh sheets on her bed just last night. "But my place wouldn't pass military inspection."

"No worries. I'm not the neat freak in my family. My…"

When he didn't finish his sentence, she glanced over her shoulder and found him frowning. *Nice going, Yates. You had a very sexy man all hot and bothered five minutes ago, then ruined the moment with your inane chatter about housekeeping.*

"Danica." His gaze bore into hers, troubled. "There's—"

"Sorry," she interrupted. "I don't know why I'd waste a single second thinking about something like laundry or dusting when I could be doing this." She stepped toward him, not stopping until their bodies touched. His hips cradled hers, the heat of him potent even through his jeans, and her breasts were cushioned against the unyielding muscular wall of his chest.

She meshed her fingers in his hair, pulling him closer. Not that it required any effort. He was already lowering his face to hers. But at the last minute, he shifted direction. Instead of meeting her lips, he kissed her jaw and worked his way down the excruciatingly sensitive line of her neck. He bit gently, then less gently, and she trembled. His hands palmed her butt, kneading, making her inwardly curse her skirt. She wanted closer contact, wanted to wrap her legs around him.

He lifted his head long enough to ask, "You're sure? That you want me?" There was an oddly vulnerable emphasis to his words, but she was too lost in sensation to analyze it.

He couldn't tell the effect he had on her? Her pulse was thundering, and she was so wet, she half expected to scent the musky perfume of her own arousal. Her voice was hoarse but audible. "Never been more sure of anything."

That was obviously the permission he'd needed. His mouth captured hers, feasting. The kiss they shared was deep and wet and gloriously carnal. Not breaking the contact between them, she shuffled back a step with vague thoughts of her bedroom on the far side of the living room. His hands fisted in the hem of her camisole. She obligingly raised her arms, ending the kiss long enough for him to lift the material over her head.

They'd moved away from the slight glow of lamplight in the doorway, but even in the shadows, Gray growled approval at the sight of her breasts covered only by pale blue demi cups. He outlined the swell of one breast, and her nipples contracted to even tighter points. She shifted her weight restlessly, slick with need. It was inexplicable, how the delicate brush of his finger over her skin could trigger such a powerful response. He circled one rigid tip, and she arched her back, reflexively offering herself up for further exploration.

But when he slid his fingers beneath the cotton of her bra, pinching lightly, it was almost too much. She nearly lost her balance.

"W-wait." Clutching his arm for support, she raised a foot and unstrapped first one high-heeled sandal, then the other. Pivoting, she kicked them under the coffee table by the couch so they weren't lying in the path to the bedroom. This evening was going to end in mind-blowing orgasms, not someone tripping over discarded shoes.

Before she could turn back around to face him, his hands settled on her denim-clad hips. He kissed his way from one shoulder blade to the other. He traced her spine to the top of her skirt, then pointedly tugged the waistband.

She reached for the button above the zipper but paused. "I feel underdressed, comparatively speaking." Twisting to look back at him, she grinned. "I'll show you mine if you show me yours."

He whipped off his shirt and balled it up, tossing it in the general vicinity of the coffee table. As he quickly stripped off socks and shoes and fumbled with his belt, she watched over her shoulder. She greedily drank in the sight of his chiseled chest and abs, cursing herself for not turning on more lights. The man was living art. His shoulders were broad and strong, his chest dusted in dark hair that added to his virile air. His torso tapered to an impressively ridged six-pack that she would have assumed was airbrushed if she'd seen it in a photo.

When he stepped out of the jeans, her eyes widened in renewed appreciation at the erection outlined in snug boxer briefs. He was male perfection. And, for tonight, he was hers.

"Your skirt," he said, his voice thick with expectation.

She gave a quick shimmy, letting the unzipped skirt slide down her legs. He hauled her closer, so that they were pressed together. She swiveled her hips, grinding against him, hearing the way he sucked in his breath, loving that his reaction to her was every bit as strong as hers to him. He reached between them to unhook her bra. Her muscles were so taut with anticipation she struggled to shrug free of the material. He skimmed his fingers over her midriff, upward. But before he reached her breasts, he changed direction. She let him get away with a second teasing pass before grabbing his hands and cupping them over her. His low chuckle, more vibration than sound, rumbled through her.

He plucked at one nipple, making her gasp. "Is that more what you had in mind?" he murmured against her ear.

Yes. She arched into his touch, words escaping her when he repeated the movement, this time tweaking both at once while he kissed her shoulder. She rocked back against him, the movement more instinct than conscious volition. He slid a hand past her hipbone, his fingers curling beneath the thin fabric of her panties to graze her skin.

She was both frantic for him to reach the throbbing juncture between her legs and a touch apprehensive that, once he did, she'd ignite like a roman candle. She had a fanciful image of herself, sated in boneless aftermath, her apartment a smoldering ruin around her. When he began lowering her panties, she had a moment of clarity.

"Condoms," she blurted. That was nonnegotiable, something they needed to agree on before either of them was fully naked.

"Of course." His acceptance was immediate, although his voice was gruff. "Jeans pocket. In a minute. First…" His fingers parted the dewy folds at her core, expertly targeting where she was most sensitive. She whimpered, moving against him with primal urgency, reaching out blindly for a way to steady herself.

He steered her toward the couch and splayed his hand on the small of her back, gently urging her forward. She bent over the arm of the sofa, the leather cool against her bare skin. He eased a finger inside her, and she bit her lip.

"Condoms," she repeated. *Now.*

"Right." His voice echoed with the same hunger surging through her.

She heard the rustle of his jeans, the thud of a wallet hitting the floor, the discreet rip of foil. His talented fingers returned, working their magic and heightening the frenzied need inside her until she almost screamed into the sofa cushion. Then he gripped her hips in a hold that bordered on bruising and thrust into her.

He withdrew partially, then pushed back even deeper. It felt so damn good. As their rhythm increased, she raised her hips to meet him, their bodies coming together with enough force to send her up on her toes. Already, a wicked, shimmering pressure was building, spreading through her body as she tightened around him. He reached around her, his fingers stroking just above where they were joined, and she cried out. The pressure broke, exploding in ripples of pleasure that radiated through every cell of her body.

Somewhere in the glittery starburst of bliss, as Gray pistoned his hips again and found his own release, she had a single coherent thought. Pretending that nothing had happened when she saw him again on Monday would be a problem. Having experienced this shattering, all-consuming ecstasy, how would she ever have a simply platonic exchange with him again?

5

SEAN CONSIDERED HIMSELF pretty fit, but right now—sprawled across Dani's couch with her tucked against him—he wasn't sure he would ever catch his breath again. Should his heart still be pounding against his rib cage? At least the spots in his vision were clearing, which made it easier to appreciate the view of the naked brunette in his arms. Technically, they were both too tall for the sofa, but even given the awkwardness of his legs hanging over the side, he was surprisingly comfortable.

Dani's head rested on his chest. She sighed happily. "That was…"

"Very athletic of us. I wonder if the Olympic committee has ever considered adding couch sex as an event."

"You'd definitely be on the medal podium."

"Both of us," he corrected. "Pairs event. Singles isn't nearly as much fun."

"Or as sweaty." She propped herself up on one arm. "I'm feeling pretty sticky. Care to join me in the shower?"

There was the slightest note of shyness in her invitation, which he found endearing. It was difficult to imagine such a forthright, sensual woman feeling bashful. But forthright didn't mean invulnerable. He recalled the flash of emotion in her gaze when she'd confessed that her ex-fiancé had eloped with someone else.

"I would love to join you, assuming I can still move." He wiggled his toes experimentally.

She unfolded herself from their tangle of limbs, raising her arms over her head and stretching her spine. Then she stood, grinning over her shoulder. "I'll try to save you some hot water, but I can't make any promises. It doesn't last long."

Watching her stroll across the room, her nude body outlined by the illumination coming through the window, helped him rediscover his energy.

She'd left her bedroom dark as she passed through, but light spilled from the bathroom. It was pretty basic—navy towels that matched small area rugs and a clear shower curtain imprinted with dark blue swirls. With the exception of the curling iron and cosmetics on the counter, he wouldn't have guessed the room belonged to a woman. His ex had fancy soaps no one was allowed to use, lace-edged washcloths and scented candles on a shelf above her tub. She'd also favored lots of sweet-smelling potpourri; visiting her apartment was like being trapped inside a raspberry. Dani didn't need pastel throw pillows or ruffled curtains to highlight her femininity—it was stamped on every curve of her body, from her lush lips to the graceful arch of her foot.

Standing beneath the spray of water, she smiled at him through the translucent curtain. "Here to wash my back?"

"Something like that." He stepped over the side of the tub, joining her.

Squeezing into the narrow bathtub was like cuddling on the couch all over again—crowded, yet not uncomfortable. He liked being here with her. *Too bad you won't be with her much longer.* The thought was a dark whisper in his mind, an unpleasant reminder that their time was limited. When he told her the truth tomorrow...

"Here." He reached for the shampoo bottle she held. "Let me." He squeezed some of the citrusy shampoo into his palm and worked it into a lather.

With the water temporarily taming her curls, her hair hung even longer than it had dry. He took his time, massaging her scalp, working the shampoo through each strand, enjoying her soft *mmm* of contentment. She was gratifyingly vocal, making it easy for a guy to tell when he was doing something right.

After he'd finished with both the shampoo and conditioner, she turned in his arms, snuggling against him as she dotted kisses along his collarbone. "That felt good. I can't remember the last time I was this relaxed."

"What can I say? Making you feel good is addictive." He tipped her chin up with his finger and kissed her. With their earlier urgency somewhat mellowed, this kiss was slow and leisurely. The sex had been incredible but, in retrospect, he wished he'd taken more time to explore her body, to find all the secret places that made her moan and writhe.

He straightened abruptly, reaching for the bottle of body oil on the shower shelf. "You know, you should never underestimate the importance of moisturizing." He started to pour the liquid into his palm, then changed his mind, drizzling it directly across her shoulders and chest.

Her earlier lassitude was gone, her dreamy expression replaced by an eager gleam in her gaze. How was it possible for someone's eyes to be so dark and so bright at the same time? He rubbed the satiny oil in lazy circles across her skin. When he caressed the undersides of her breasts, her head fell back, lips parted on a noiseless sigh.

He brushed a thumb over one taut peak. "I didn't get the chance, earlier, to taste you here." An oversight he meant to correct immediately. He bent his head, swirling his tongue around her nipple, then sucking hard.

She made a sound low in her throat that reverberated off the tile walls. If it weren't for his realization that the water pelting his skin was turning increasingly cool, he could happily stay here for hours. Reluctantly, he let her go.

"You weren't kidding about the short-lived hot water," he complained. "If we don't get out of here, we're going to turn into popsicles."

"Told you," she said ruefully. As she drew back the shower curtain, she added, "It's probably just as well. I'm starting to get light-headed from hunger. Not that I was thinking about food while you were... With your mouth on me, I can't think at all."

"We'll have to test that theory later. There are other places I still haven't had the chance to kiss you," he drawled, his voice full of wicked intent.

She stilled, her eyes wide and her cheeks rosy with color. It took considerable willpower not to scoop her up and carry her to the bed in the next room. But then she blinked, shaking off her reverie and grabbing an oversize blue towel. She handed him a matching one.

Wrapping herself in terry cloth, she tucked in the corner so that it formed a mini-dress. "I really am starving. Three beers and a handful of chips does not a dinner make."

"You sure?" He secured his own towel around his waist. "I have a number of buddies who would consider that fine dining."

"I just hope I have actual groceries. I put in what feels like a hundred hours of work this week."

Including going to the office on a Saturday. "Are you always so driven, or were you going out of your way to stay busy?" he asked tactfully. The days leading up to the aborted wedding must have been tough.

"Both. My colleagues call me ambitious."

He managed not to wince at the word. Once she knew more about him, would she share his ex's opinion—that Sean was going nowhere simply because he didn't wear expensive suits to work? He was currently the lead builder on a new phase of a luxury subdivision. He'd worked before in brick and concrete neighborhoods where every house looked alike and the only landscaping attention was given to the token shrubbery surrounding the pool area and private tennis courts. This subdivision, on the other hand, had personality in addition to the community pool and clubhouse. Flowering magnolia and dogwood trees offered shade and color in generous-size yards; stately pines marched along property lines. It struck him as the kind of dream neighborhood his parents would have loved to raise him and Bryce in, had they ever been able to afford it.

"I've always been goal oriented," Dani continued as

she flipped on her bedroom light. "And I don't mind busting my ass to meet those goals." She shot him a grin. "But I try not to let it make me stuffy."

"Definitely *not* the word I would use to describe you."

Her apartment was so small there was no hallway. The living room sat in the center, with a kitchen and bedroom at either end. Now that there were more lights on, he was getting his first real look at the place. A flat-screen television hung on the wall, above a shelf of DVDs. Most of the titles he glimpsed were action movies.

"You bowl?" he asked, spotting a turquoise bowling bag in the corner.

"It used to be a weekly tradition for me and my dad. He gave me a ball for my birthday a few years back, but it's been a while."

"That him?" Sean asked, noting the framed eight-by-ten on a small end table. It looked pretty recent. Sean knew the stern-jawed man with silver hair was her father even before she nodded. The man had the same dark eyes as his daughter—and the same air of determination.

"Yep, that's the Major," she said, affectionate pride in her voice.

In the kitchen, a couple more photos were stuck to the refrigerator with pizza delivery magnets. One was a shot of Dani in a tank top and sunglasses, a runner's number pinned to her shirt.

"Last year's Peachtree Road Race," she said, following his gaze. "The other one's me and my friend Meg."

The two women sat on the deck of a boat, crossing their eyes comically and raising bottles of beer.

"She barely looks old enough to drink," he commented. "Or...I don't know." It wasn't that the pretty woman literally looked underage. It was more a sense of innocence and youthful merriment. Strawberry-blond ringlets framed a cherubic face with a button nose, a smattering of freckles and a sweet smile. "If I had to guess, I'd say she either teaches kindergarten or directs a church choir. Maybe both."

"She owns a high-end lingerie store and sells the occasional sex toy at private parties."

While he absorbed that bombshell, Dani added, "I actually need to send her a quick text to let her know I, uh, got home okay. Excuse me for a sec?" She retrieved her cell phone from the purse she'd dropped as soon as they entered the apartment.

Sean continued his informal study of her place. Her personal mementos seemed limited to the three pictures he'd seen. Because she wasn't overly sentimental, or because she'd removed any keepsakes that included her ex? Sean had an irrational urge to punch the unknown former fiancé in the nose. He hated the idea of any guy hurting her.

"Okay. Food," Dani said decisively. She swung open the refrigerator door, frowned at the array of takeout containers, then checked the freezer.

Watching over her shoulder, Sean laughed. "Takeout food, beer and pizzas? You have the body of a swimsuit model, but the refrigerator of a frat house."

She raised an eyebrow. "Oh, and I suppose *your* fridge is full of kale and imported brie?"

"Touché."

The kitchen was small enough that Dani could preheat the oven without even stepping away from the fridge. She pulled a square box from the freezer. "I doubt college boys splurge on gourmet Mediterranean veggie pizzas. This okay with you?"

He nodded. Although he hadn't given food much thought before she mentioned it, now he realized he was famished, too.

She opened an overhead cabinet, which caused her towel to slip a tantalizing half inch, and got down two glasses. "Help yourself to anything you want to drink."

He waited until she was done with the pitcher of filtered water, then poured himself a glass, as well. The digital display signaled that the oven was preheated, and she set the pizza on the rack.

"Frozen pizza and a dress code of towels." She grinned at him as she set the timer on the microwave. "Do I know how to throw a classy dinner party or what?"

"Best social event I've been to all year. And, trust me, I was dragged to plenty." He hadn't meant to add that part, but it was true. Tara had the busiest calendar of anyone he'd ever known.

"Work events?"

"No. Ex-girlfriend, hell-bent on networking." Looking back, he was surprised he'd convinced the youngest daughter of Dunwoody socialites to go out with him in the first place. "You're not the only one who's been through a breakup recently," he commiserated.

"Were the two of you serious?"

"There was a time I thought we might be, but we never lived together or got engaged." He could imagine the disdain on Tara's face if he'd proposed. "She wanted someone different. Or at least, she wanted me to be someone different."

"Then she's a moron. You're…" She ducked her gaze. "Well. You're you."

Under other circumstances, the soft spoken flattery would have gone straight to his head. But it was impossible to accept the compliment when she didn't know who he was. *Doesn't she?* She'd spent hours with him, enjoying his company and their chemistry. Okay, she had his name wrong, but was that more important than the connection they'd formed?

"So did you always know you wanted to be an architect?" she asked.

He flinched inwardly, her innocuous question destroying his attempt at rationalization. "Not exactly," he said. "I got started in my dad's roofing company. I guess my career evolved from there. You spend enough time working on people's houses you start to imagine how you would build them yourself. What you'd do differently. What your own dream home might be like." That was entirely true. He might not have Bryce's schooling, but Sean had consulted with friends and experts and was almost finished with blueprints for his eventual dream home.

"Sounds a little like my inspiration. Except I never worked as a roofer."

"Shame. You'd look cute in a hard hat."

"Dad and I moved a bunch of times when I was growing up, so I spent a lot of time daydreaming about my perfect home, too. In case you were wondering," she added in a wry voice, "this apartment isn't it. This was just a temporary stop that got extended when my relationship status changed. Anyway, even when Dad and I stayed in a place longer than usual, it was base housing. It was never truly *ours*. Helping clients find their perfect place makes me feel like a fairy godmother."

He tilted his head, unable to reconcile the sexy as hell woman whose towel only barely concealed her luscious breasts with a kindly old godmother. "Didn't you want to be the princess when you were a little girl?" Dani was certainly more beautiful than any fabled heroine with snowy skin or rosy lips.

She snorted. "Princesses hid out with dwarves or waited around in towers. The really unlucky ones waited around in comas. Fairy godmothers get shit *done*." She opened a drawer, pulling out a pizza cutter and brandishing it like a magic wand. "And I'd be effective, too. None of this spells wearing off at midnight nonsense."

That, he could believe. Because he felt as if he'd been bewitched since the moment she first smiled at him, and the spell she cast over him had been growing steadily stronger ever since.

WHEN DANI STOOD to refill her water, she caught a glance at the time. She blinked, startled by the numbers glowing above her microwave. Had she and Gray really just spent an hour and a half sitting on the floor of her kitchen? They'd wiped out the pizza amid conversation and far more laughter than she'd expected.

In some ways, being with him reminded her of hanging out with Meg. Her best friend was usually the only person who could bring out Dani's silly side. Major Yates had many excellent parenting qualities, but her childhood home hadn't been filled with carefree whimsy. One of the traits she found attractive in Gray was that he didn't take himself too seriously.

Apparently, though, it was true what they said about time flying when you were having fun.

"It's late," she told him.

He glanced up, his eyes searching. "Is that your way of suggesting it's time for me to leave?"

"No, I... Stay the night? I've got spare toothbrushes." A hot blush prickled her skin as she realized how that—coupled with propositioning him after three minutes of small talk today—might make her sound. "I bought a multipack because it was on sale. Not, uh, because I have guys sleeping over on a regular basis."

"I'd love to stay, Dani."

The way he said her name made her melt inside. But when she caught herself gazing adoringly at him, she gave herself a mental shake. Sappy wasn't her thing. "I'll, uh, just go find you that extra toothbrush."

She retreated to the bathroom, taking time to recover her composure. She ran a comb through her hair, brushed her teeth and finally exchanged the towel she'd been wearing for a robe from Meg's shop. The green material was filmy, almost but not quite see-through, and fell to midthigh. When she opened the door, she found Gray sitting on the edge of her bed in nothing but his boxer briefs. Since she'd had all evening to get used to the sight of his well-muscled torso, it was silly that her mouth went dry. It was equally silly that her stomach did a somersault at *Gray* and *bed* in the same thought. Didn't sexual tension fade after two people had been intimate? Shouldn't his magnetism have lessened?

No. Because now you know exactly how good he is. All her feverish speculation before had only been educated guesses.

She swallowed, struggling to find her voice. Although she hadn't wanted him to think she picked up a different man every night of the week, she didn't want him to deem her unsophisticated, either. Then again, considering her abysmal language whenever she missed a pool shot and the contents of her fridge, that ship had probably sailed.

"Um, all yours," she said, moving out of the doorway. While Gray took his turn in the bathroom, she sent one last check-in text to Meg.

He's staying over. Best date ever. Call you tomorrow.

When Gray rejoined her, she was in the process of turning down the comforter. "Two things you should know," she said with mock solemnity. "The right side of the bed is mine. Nonnegotiable. Also, I snore." She had no idea if that was true. But making the statement kept her from swooning over his body. Any man who ate pizza and had abs like that must've signed a deal with the devil.

"Hmm." He reached across the bed for her, eyes glinting with sensual promise. "Then maybe I should come up with ways to keep you awake, so the snoring won't be a problem."

A quiver of expectation rippled through her. She met him in the middle of the mattress. After only one night, his kiss was familiar, as if they were lovers with a shared past. *And a future?* It was a sweet thought, but fleeting, incinerated by the rush of fiery need as their tongues tangled. He tunneled his fingers through her hair, which had dried in wild ringlets that matched her mood. Untamed. Primitive.

Using the element of surprise as much as her own

weight, she shoved him back onto the bed and sprawled across him as they kissed. He cupped her ass through the silky material, dragging her against him. She sat up, straddling him, so that she could control her movements better.

"I like this," he said. "But—"

"There's a *but*?" Was he one of those men who had a problem with a woman on top? *Nah.* He was rock hard beneath her, obviously sincere in his appreciation. She shifted her weight in a slow, deliberate gyration.

He closed his eyes momentarily, his grip on her tightening. "But," he continued, "we still have a theory to test." That was all the warning he gave before flipping her over and reversing their positions. "About my mouth on you."

His weight on top of her, wedged between her thighs as he pinned her to the crisp sheets below, was a new erotic delight. He caught the end of the sash belting her robe and tugged. The knot gave way immediately, and the fabric parted, sliding down either side of her body.

But he kept his eyes locked on hers as he whispered, "You are beautiful." Something about the reverence of his tone more than the actual words made her shiver.

Kissing her neck, he scraped his teeth lightly across the hollow of her throat and nuzzled his way downward. By the time he reached the tip of her breast, she was breathing hard. He flicked his tongue over her, then drew her into the heat of his mouth. It was as if there was a current that ran from his lips straight to the core of her.

Electric pleasure zinged through her body until she was shuddering with it. If he'd continued his attention to her breasts, it might have been enough to push her over the edge into climax. But he was moving lower, stopping to kiss her navel, both her inner thighs. And then finally, *finally…*

"Oh!" The soft exclamation was all she could manage.

Hands beneath her knees, he nudged gently, and she bent her legs, resting her feet against his shoulders. Coherent thought evaporated beneath the stroke of his tongue. Her head thrashed on the pillow, and her heels dug into the mattress. The neighbors could probably hear the sharp cries Gray wrung from her, but she was beyond caring.

Then it was as if all motion and sound stopped. Her body straightened, a silent gasp frozen on her lips, and spasms began deep within her, undulating through her in crashing waves. It took her a moment to register that Gray's sudden absence was because he was unrolling a condom. She was still experiencing tiny aftershocks when he braced himself above her and drove into her, hurtling her up another roller-coaster ascent toward free fall.

She lifted her head, planning to kiss him, but their gazes locked, as intimately joined as their bodies. Looking into his face, she knew this was the closest she'd ever felt to another person. And even though the realization was a little scary, she was almost certain he felt the same way.

SEAN WOKE LANGUOROUSLY from a dead sleep. Before he was awake enough to form thoughts, he was only aware of a bone-deep contentment and the lush female body curled against him, her skin warm and smooth. *Dani.*

He opened his eyes to check the time, and the sunshine flooding her room was like an accusation. Their night together had long since passed. In the dark, he'd almost convinced himself he could give her enough pleasure to atone for his lie of omission. Now he had to face her in the light of day—and face up to what he'd done.

"Mornin'." Her drowsy voice was a purr of greeting as she affectionately wriggled against him.

He should be worn out from the previous night, but his body, seemingly oblivious to his moral plight, was already responding.

Irritated with his lack of self-discipline, he jerked away from her. "Good morning."

His brusque words were met with an odd stillness. He could almost see her unspoken questions forming in the air.

"Sorry. I'm a bear in the morning." He climbed out of the bed to get some distance between them. That last time they'd made love, something had changed. Shifted. He couldn't touch her now, not until she knew the truth. "You have a coffeemaker?"

She nodded, eyeing him warily but no longer frowning. "I'm more of a tea drinker myself, but I keep coffee in the cabinet for company. There's a sugar bowl on the counter, and about a fifty-fifty chance the milk in the fridge hasn't expired."

"I'm going to get a pot started. Be back in a couple of minutes." And, hopefully, between now and then, he'd figure out a way to explain his identity that wouldn't make her hate him forever.

6

DANI HAD HEARD of awkward mornings after, but this was more like a complete personality transplant. What was wrong with him? He said he was cranky in the mornings, which maybe explained his tone, but why wouldn't he meet her eyes? What had happened to the man who'd laughed with her last night and confided in her? The one who'd made love to her until she was limp with satisfaction? In her experience, it was a major warning sign when a guy started acting jumpy, his behavior erratic.

Gray is not *your low-life ex. Don't overreact.*

With weeks of looking back on her engagement to give her perspective, she'd realized that Tate had a nasty, yet subtle, habit of belittling her. Literally, in the case of cajoling her not to wear high heels. He was the kind of man who sulked when he lost and liked people around him to be a tiny bit weaker so that he appeared stronger in comparison. Gray was far more secure than that. He'd seemed genuinely delighted at having serious competition when they played pool, and he hadn't cringed once at her "unladylike" language.

As for being with a strong woman? If she told Gray she wanted to handcuff him to her headboard and have her way with him, she suspected he'd be all for it. At least, the lover who'd ravished her last night would have been. She was less sure about the man who'd recoiled from her this morning.

Listening to his footsteps as he padded back to the room, it occurred to her that she was completely naked. Granted, he'd already seen everything there was to see, but she was suddenly feeling a lot more inhibited. Vulnerable. Who knew where her discarded robe had ended up? She quickly wound the sheet around her, six-hundred-thread-count makeshift armor.

Far from looking more alert or bolstered by the prospect of imminent coffee, when Gray returned, he was even more grim faced. He'd pulled on his jeans, and she found herself wishing he'd put on his shirt, too. This didn't seem like a good time to get distracted by his sculpted chest.

She wasn't one to beat around the bush, and the experience with Tate had taught her to trust her instincts even when she didn't like what they were telling her. "What's the problem?"

Staring at the floor, he inhaled deeply, then blew out his breath. "I need to tell you something, but it's tough to explain." He finally met her eyes, but the uneasiness in his gaze wasn't comforting. The dark stubble shadowing his jaw—albeit sexy in a scruffy way—added to the sense that he'd somehow transformed into a stranger, far removed from the polished architect she was used to seeing. "What I'm about to say doesn't have to change anything, Dani."

He's lying. "You ever notice how prefacing bad news

with 'don't panic' causes panic?" She was impressed she sounded so calm, no tremor to betray the dread coiled like a snake in the pit of her stomach. "Or how people who start, 'No offense…' are about to say something offensive?" Whatever he was about to say, she was willing to bet it was a game changer.

"When I saw you yesterday," he said, "I felt an instant flare of attraction. You felt it, too."

She cocked her head to the side, puzzled by the defensive undercurrent in his tone. Why did it sound as if he were trying to justify what had happened between them? They were consenting adults, and there was no reason she could think of for him to feel guilty about it. Unless… "That ex you mentioned? Is she maybe not as *ex* as you suggested?" If he'd gone home with Dani without first ending a bad relationship, she didn't know if she could forgive him, not when she knew what it was like to be cheated on firsthand.

"What? No! This doesn't have anything to do with Tara. This is about…my brother. We used to be really close, but we're very different people. I make spontaneous—sometimes regrettable—decisions, and he plans out every choice he makes. He doesn't do impulsive things like follow a beautiful stranger in need of a good time to a bar."

Why was he babbling about his brother? Perhaps she'd been too quick to assure Meg she hadn't gone home with a psycho. Wild-eyed and off on a tangent, he seemed less mentally stable.

He sat on the edge of the bed, close but not touching her. "My brother is an architect. In your building."

"You're both architects?" Wait. Why call it her building when he worked there, too?

"No, just him. His name is Bryce Grayson. He works for Bertram Design Associates."

"*His* name is Bryce?" She scrambled backward until she bumped the headboard, trying to decide if she was dealing with some bizarre multiple personality thing. Or if he was secretly employed by one of those reality shows that messed with people's minds. "You're Bryce Grayson."

He shook his head. "I'm his twin brother. Sean."

Holy hell, she'd seduced a total stranger. A liar, at that. She shot out of the bed, mind reeling. Bryce had an evil twin? Impossible. That was the kind of thing that happened in freaking soap operas, not real life.

Gray—Sean?—stood, too, his eyes beseeching. "When you first asked me to join you for that drink, to help you let off some steam, I had no idea you thought I was him."

"And as soon as you realized?"

He glanced away, guilt and misery marring his breathtaking profile. For an inane moment, she wanted to reach for him, comfort him.

But then anger rose, a dark tide. "Did you think I was so desperate to get laid that I wouldn't care who I screwed?" she bit out. "Or were you afraid I wasn't desperate enough, that I'd walk away if I knew you weren't the man I wanted?"

His eyes flashed, her words riling him past contrition. "I *am* the man you wanted. You had hours to be sure of that before you brought me back here. And you can't tell me you know Bryce any better than that. Before yesterday, the two of you had never even exchanged names."

The truth in his words didn't come close to extinguishing her rage. If anything, it infuriated her more. "Don't try to defend what you did! I just got out of a very long relationship with a liar. I am not about to get involved with another one. Get out of my apartment."

"Danica—"

"Out," she said coldly. She was working so hard to control her temper, afraid that if she let it loose, she'd find herself in the midst of an honest to God tantrum, throwing her belongings and risking her security deposit.

He stared her down. For a second, she thought he might continue pleading his case.

His shoulders sagged in defeat. He gave her one last look and returned to the living room, where his shoes and shirt were. Apparently, he didn't even bother to put them on, merely scooped them up, because bare seconds later her front door opened, then clicked shut with gut-wrenching finality.

Dani pressed her hands to her midsection, not sure if she was going to cry or throw up. An image from last night taunted her, his eyes peering down at her as they moved together. She recalled sardonically how close she'd felt to him. And she hadn't even known his *name*. His bizarre announcement this morning left her feeling as blindsided as she had the day Tate called off their engagement—maybe more. At least with Tate, there had been some suspicion, some minor foreshadowing.

What was wrong with her? Was she inherently attracted to dishonest men?

Were there any honest ones?

Blood pressure skyrocketing, she scrambled for her cell phone. Meg answered a moment later.

"Thank goodness you called," her friend burbled. "I didn't want to, you know, interrupt anything, but

I have been dying of curiosity! Tell me all about the 'best date ever.'"

Not a date, a con. She opened her mouth to say as much, to spew venom and call Sean Grayson every bad word she knew, but, to her horror, only a sob emerged.

"Oh, honey." Meg's cheerful tone immediately switched to concern. "I was hoping a wild night with Hot Architect would be enough to erase Tate from your memory."

Architect? Good Lord. She had no idea what the guy did for a living.

"But I guess," Meg continued, "with it being the weekend of your wedding, it's only—"

"I am not upset about the wedding. Or Tate." She was far too ticked off at Sean to give a damn about the man she was supposed to have exchanged vows with yesterday. Was that the secret to getting over an ex once and for all, finding someone else who enraged you even more? If so, all she needed now was to go out with a guy who stole her car and burned down her apartment, and maybe she could put this latest mistake behind her, too.

Shouldn't be a problem. With her crappy judgment in men, she'd be dating a felon in no time.

DEEMING THE STORY too surreal to be discussed over the phone, Meg came over, bringing with her a jug of orange juice and a bottle of champagne. "At this hour, I figured our only acceptable options were mimosas or Bloody Marys."

"I'll get cups," Dani said. She'd taken a quick shower, trying not to recall the tenderness with which Sean had washed her hair or the heat of his mouth on her, and changed into yoga pants and a funny T-shirt Meg had given her to make her laugh after the breakup with Tate.

Now, her vision blurred as gratitude swamped her. "What would I do without you? Every time I get screwed over, you come pick up the pieces."

Meg squeezed her shoulder. "You've done the same for me more times than I want to think about." Her luck with men had not been stellar. Some guys were scared off by her effusive personality. Others were attracted to her wholesome appearance and tendency to use exclamations like "fudge!" but felt deceived when they glimpsed her naughtier side.

Dani frequently teased her friend for her use of G-rated substitute expletives. Meg said it had become a lifelong habit because her mother took serious offense to swearing and in a home with five kids, there was always someone waiting to tell on you. "So you won't say *hell*," Dani had asked once, "but your mom is okay with you and your sister running a store filled with sexy items?"

"My parents aren't prudes. How do you think they got the five kids?"

It was starting to feel like a miracle to Dani that any couple stayed together long enough to have five kids. Two man disasters in the space of a month was a new record. Meg had been putting in a lot of overtime lately in the cheering-up department.

"Seriously," Dani said, "I owe you. I'm beginning to feel like our friendship is one-sided."

"You don't owe me anything. Being your friend is its own reward." Meg gave her a wry smile. "Plus, your life is never dull. Who would have guessed Hot Architect had a Hot Twin?"

Not me. In retrospect, she felt stupid. Hadn't she subconsciously catalogued the ways Sean seemed different, from his unexpectedly outgoing manner to his biceps? But as an only child herself, she'd never given any consideration to whether Bryce had siblings, much less one who was identical.

She and Meg took their champagne-heavy cocktails into the living room, where Dani sat as far from the couch as possible and explained what she could. There were some blanks only Sean could have filled in— such as what he'd been doing at his brother's office on a Saturday afternoon in the first place. By the time she'd shared as many of the details as she could bear repeating, they were on their second round of mimosas.

Meg had kicked off her shoes and sat with her legs tucked under her. "I wonder if he's done it before, pretended to be his brother. Some sets of twins think it's funny to swap places and prank other people."

"What happened between us went beyond a 'prank,'" Dani said stiffly, recalling how foolishly close she'd felt to him. She honestly wasn't sure what ticked her off more, his dishonesty or how dumb she'd been.

Time to use your brains, Yates. A smart woman wouldn't spend another second dwelling on last night or the way he'd touched her. The way he'd coaxed her into laughing and revealing silly anecdotes. The way he'd—

No more! Kicking him out of her thoughts might not be as easy as kicking him out of her apartment this morning, but she would manage it. After all, she was pretty sure that a guy hard-hearted enough to lie about his identity just to get some action wasn't giving *her* a second thought.

BY LATE AFTERNOON, Sean had concluded he couldn't stand his own company. Being cooped up with the memory of Dani's stricken expression as she'd ordered him to leave was making him nuts. He called several buddies to see if he could get a poker night going or if anyone wanted to catch the latest spy thriller on the big screen. But all he got were apologies, rain checks and voice-mail recordings. Finally, he stalked out of his town house with no real idea of where he was headed.

Part of him wanted to go straight back to Dani's place, to apologize again now that she'd had a few hours to get past her initial shock. But maybe it would be better to approach her at a neutral location, like her office building. She was predisposed to think badly of him right now. If he confronted her at home, she might decide he was a stalker. He'd shredded her opinion of him enough for one day.

Would she be better off if she'd encountered the real Bryce Grayson yesterday? Bryce wouldn't have gone home with her, but he wouldn't have lied to her, either, wouldn't have put that wounded anger in her eyes. Maybe because Sean was thinking of his brother, or maybe because their shared birthday was tomorrow, he soon found himself rolling up to the security gate at Bryce's condominium. He punched in the security code, wondering if his brother was even at home.

Only one way to find out.

"Sean?" Bryce swung open his front door, his tone confused.

Whatever Sean might have said in greeting disappeared when he noticed the crisp white dress shirt his brother wore with black suit pants. An unknotted bowtie hung around his collar. "You always dress like a 007 wannabe on Sunday afternoons?"

His brother narrowed his eyes, taking in the rumpled T-shirt that had spent all week in the dryer and jeans that were threadbare at the knees. "Criticism from the man who looks like he slept in his clothes?"

Actually, I slept naked. In Dani's arms. Misery clogged his throat, and he swallowed hard. "I need to talk to you." Just as it would have been unconscionable to let Dani run into his twin without first telling her the truth, he should come clean with his brother.

"I'm leaving in the next fifteen minutes," Bryce said, checking his watch. "The firm is hosting a table at a charity auction tonight."

"Can I come in if I promise to make it brief?" Maybe a limited amount of time was best. Fifteen minutes probably wasn't long enough for Bryce to kill him and convincingly stage it to look like an accident.

"All right." Bryce stepped aside, his expression impatient.

The open floor plan of the loft made it seem huge. Gleaming hardwood stretched from the front door to the exposed brick of the back wall. When their mom had badgered Bryce into letting them use the place for their dad's surprise birthday party, Tara had been effusive over Bryce's posh surroundings and view of the Atlanta skyline.

Frowning at the wall opposite them, Sean noticed the expanse of glossy white was broken only by hooks and nails. The framed pictures and set of shelves that had previously hung there were propped against the baseboard below.

"I'm making room for the painting I'm buying. At the auction," Bryce said, a pointed reminder that he had somewhere to be.

How like Bryce. Not only did he know exactly what he planned to bid on, he'd already decided he was going to win. Hell, maybe he would. *He* wasn't the family screwup.

Sean took a deep breath. "It's about a woman."

"Tara?"

"No, we broke up last month." Although Sean didn't speak directly to his brother often, their mom tried to keep everyone updated on family gossip. But she'd been busy preparing for an eleven-night cruise to Hawaii. They wouldn't be back until the end of the week. "It's actually a woman who works in your building. Danica…um, about yea tall? Gorgeous brunette, real-estate agent down the hall from you."

"Oh." Bryce nodded. "Right. I know who you're talking about."

His brother's offhand tone made Sean angry on Dani's behalf. What had she said when she thought he was Bryce? *I've been thinking about you all week.* She'd noticed Bryce, wanted him. As much as the idea of her desiring his brother put Sean's teeth on edge, it was almost worse that Bryce had barely registered her existence. She was stunning, special. She deserved a man who—

Who what? Lies to her? Cold reality sliced through his righteous indignation. Last night, he'd wanted to take a swing at her ex-fiancé, wanted to sock the guy in the nose for hurting her. *Congratulations, now you're the guy hurting her.* He was in the mood for a fight, but it was difficult to kick one's own ass.

Maybe after he admitted to Bryce what he'd done, his big brother would take care of that for him.

7

BRYCE GRAYSON WAS having trouble following the conversation. He was still trying to adjust to the surprise of finding Sean on his doorstep.

In the entire time Bryce had lived in the loft, his brother had never once dropped by out of the blue. Why would he? Sean had plenty of friends to call when he wanted to hang out; it had been that way since grade school. Bryce, as the twin their parents had always relied on to follow the rules, was more successful in relationships with clear protocols—it was one of the reasons he'd joined a fraternity. From pledging to initiation, there were conventions to follow.

Sean didn't need convention. And he'd never needed help with women before, either, so Bryce doubted his brother was here to ask for an introduction to the brunette he'd mentioned.

He fastened a cuff link, hoping Sean reached his point soon. Punctuality was one of those social conventions Bryce respected. "What does this Danica have to do with anything?"

"I met her in your office building yesterday. We went

out last night…but she thought I was you. I, um, didn't correct her."

"What?" Bryce jerked his head up sharply. "You let her think she was on a date with me?"

"It's complicated."

"It's identity theft!"

Sean rolled his eyes. "It's not like I took your credit cards to Vegas."

No, this was far worse! As a kid, Sean had been the type to throw a football in the house, then have the nerve to look shocked when something got broken. Although Bryce no longer knew his brother well, it seemed as though Sean hadn't changed. He was still charismatic, impulsive and heedless of consequences.

Bryce had been the worrier. In younger years, he'd worried about his brother getting hurt doing stupid stunts. But by the time Bryce got tested into gifted classes in middle school, their formerly laconic father had given him new focus for his worry. His dad's favorite conversational theme became the opportunities that would be available if Bryce worked hard enough. Bryce began to feel as if he was shouldering the weight of his family—his mom had never gone to college, and his father only had a vocational degree. While Sean spent his high school years making out with cheerleaders, Bryce was studying for Advance Placement exams, obsessed with not losing his GPA lead to the salutatorian right on his heels.

"I didn't set out to lie to her," Sean defended himself, as if that somehow made anything better. "It happened fast. She was supposed to get married yesterday, but the cheating jerk bailed on her. She was looking for someone to… You would have been all wrong for her! It's like Tara used to say—"

"Tara your ex?" His brain hurt. Had his brother descended into daytime drinking? This exchange was making less and less sense.

Nodding, Sean glowered. "She made a point of frequently mentioning that you're the successful one, the college-educated architect with the bright future."

"So you picked up a woman in my name out of some kind of petty resentment?"

"Of course not! You don't understand—"

"What sane person could? You've done some reckless shit, but this borders on criminal." The thought of trying to make small talk with Danica after his brother's inexplicable fraud made his stomach tighten. Sean might never have to deal with her again, but Bryce crossed paths with her on a nearly daily basis. "I have to face this woman! Did that even occur to you?"

"No. I admit, I wasn't thinking about you while staring into a beautiful woman's eyes. But I figure it balances out, since you think about yourself enough for the both of us."

Bryce's fists clenched at his sides. "What the hell does that mean?"

"It means, you're a lot more concerned about climbing the ladder of success than the people you left behind. Like our parents—"

"*I'm* the one who paid to upgrade their cruise!"

"Yeah, you threw money at them," Sean retorted, "like one of the charities you support in the name of networking. How many times have you backed out of family plans because of something 'important' like this damn auction?"

Bryce had never been closer to hitting a person. "It must be so easy to stand in judgment when you weren't the one expected to succeed." How dare his jackass brother accuse him of not caring about their family? Why did Sean think he'd come back to Georgia? *The problem with Sean is, he* doesn't *think*.

"No," Sean said softly, "I guess I wouldn't know what that was like." He raked a hand through his hair. "I didn't come here to fight. I know I screwed up, and I figured I owed you the truth."

"And Danica? She deserves the truth, too." Bryce sure didn't want to be the one to explain the whole mess to her.

"I told her first thing this morning."

First thing? "Are you saying you spent the night with her?" Bryce asked, appalled.

Sean didn't reply, but the guilt in his gaze and tic in his jaw were answer enough.

Another question occurred to Bryce as his brother reached for the door. "What were you doing at my office in the first place?"

"Birthday surprise." Sean flashed a grim smile over his shoulder. "Believe it or not, I walked into that building with the best of intentions."

He'd somehow turned a token birthday gesture into a sex scandal? *Only my brother.* "In the future, do us both a favor and just send an e-card."

DANI'S MONDAY DID not get off to an auspicious start. After a fitful night of tossing and turning, only managing to drift off an hour before dawn, she overslept. Then she lost more time applying heavier makeup than normal in an attempt to cover the dark circles beneath her eyes. Naturally, she hit every red light possible on her way to work. She arrived at the office twenty minutes late. Which, for her, was like an hour late.

"Aw, sweetie." Behind her retro cat's-eye glasses, the receptionist gazed at her with blatant pity. "Tough weekend, huh?"

Crap. *So much for the concealing power of cosmetics.* "Didn't get a lot of sleep," Dani admitted. Saturday night, she'd been too busy having enthusiastic sex. Last night? She'd lain in bed plagued by memories of the enthusiastic sex. And it wasn't as if she could escape the mental replay by sleeping on her couch. Hell, she'd even thought of Sean while standing in the shower this morning, recalling the way he'd—

"Hon, you want me to hold your calls for a little while?" Although Judy was barely forty, nowhere near old enough to be Dani's mom, she had a naturally maternal air. "Give you a chance to get your bearings?"

"Thanks, Judy, but I'll be okay."

"You sure? It must be hard, being here when you're supposed to be on your honeymoon right now."

A brittle laugh escaped Dani. She kept forgetting people expected her to be upset about the wedding. She'd done some soul-searching after Meg left yesterday and had reached an epiphany. If she and Tate hadn't been on separate continents, they would have broken up much sooner. The geographic distance between them had allowed them to ignore the personality clashes and the small, grating ways in which they weren't compatible. She still thought he was slime for being unfaithful before ending their relationship, but she could honestly say he'd done her a favor by calling off the wedding.

Look at you, being all philosophical and emotion-

ally mature. Maybe there would come a day when she could view Sean Grayson's actions with such a forgiving eye. In about ninety years or so.

"Oh, I almost forgot." Judy snapped her fingers. "Your dad called first thing and asked if I could remind you about your dinner date today. I was surprised he called the office number instead of phoning you directly, but he said something's wrong with your cell?"

Dani sighed. "I was ducking calls this weekend."

"Understandable. Can I get you anything? Coffee, glass of water? Some of those miniature chocolate bars we all steal from the jar on Spencer's desk?"

"Thanks," she said, heading toward her office, "but I don't need anything." Except a time machine. What were the chances the receptionist had one of those handy? *I should check the supply closet.*

Dani wanted to go back to Saturday afternoon, when she'd been working alone in the office. If she had it all to do over again, she'd leave the building five minutes later. Or five minutes earlier. Either way worked as long as she could avoid Sean's alluring smile and captivating blue eyes.

Ironically, being with him had been part of what helped her see Tate had never been right for her. There was too much contrast between the two men, too much difference in her reaction and her comfort level. If she ever tried to settle down again—a prospect that now made her shudder—it should be with someone who made her laugh. And her toes curl. She'd always thought her sex life with Tate was adequate, if a bit conventional, but if you were going to spend the rest of your life being monogamous, shouldn't it be with someone who left you breathless?

Not necessarily. Not if the trade-off is that he's also an unscrupulous liar.

She was grateful when her phone rang, giving her a different outlet for her focus. "Danica Yates, speaking."

"Erik Frye," the attorney on the other end of the phone identified himself. "You know, the guy who's going to dominate in fantasy baseball."

She laughed. "Yeah, yeah. That's what you said about your fantasy football team, and we both know how that turned out. What have you got for me this morning?"

He updated her on the title work that had been done on a property, assuring her that the check hadn't revealed any red flags, and confirmed the time of a closing this week. He concluded the call with, "Looking forward to seeing you Wednesday afternoon."

Hanging up the phone, she sighed. Why couldn't she have developed an attraction to Erik instead of the architect down the hall? Erik was a decent guy, smart with a nice smile, not noticeably shorter than she was. He'd been divorced for a little over a year; he and his wife, also a lawyer, maintained an amicable relationship. Life would be simpler if she'd decided to go out with Friendly Attorney.

But, no. You had to lust after the unattainable hottie. She was not looking forward to bumping into Bryce. Even knowing that he had nothing to do with what had happened, it would be weird to face someone who looked just like Sean.

"You busy?" Renee Lloyd, the head licensed broker, poked her head into the office. She was a dynamic redhead with big presence. When Dani stood right next to her, she was always surprised anew that she was nearly a foot taller.

"Always. But never too busy for you."

Chuckling, Renee entered the office. "Good answer. Couple of things. Sonia Donavan is going to call you. She and I have done several commercial deals together, but now she needs someone who specializes in residential. She and her husband are divorcing and need to sell their house. Also, can we count you in again this summer as an assistant coach?" This would be the fourth year running that they'd sponsored a girls' softball team.

"Absolutely." Part of networking and building their names in the community was being an active part of the community. Some of the other agents, especially ones who had their own kids with active sports schedules, grumbled about the extra hours, but Dani looked at it as a perk of the job.

"Oh, and Magnolia Grove is opening a model home this week," Renee added. "Two different floor plans should be available in the next couple of months. Great location and school district."

Dani nodded. From what she'd heard, a lot of the houses in the first phase of the subdivision had been purchased directly through the builder. Now the second phase was under way. Visiting the neighborhood was on her to-do list, as was familiarizing herself with the builder's preregistration policy. She'd heard tales from old-school brokers about adversarial relationships with builders, but that hadn't been her experience. Renee frequently reminded them that the more people they got along with, the more sales they closed.

"I'm planning to stop by the subdivision this week," Dani said.

"Great. I'll let you get back to work, then. Watch for an email from Spencer with the softball schedule."

Dani had about an hour to spend on paperwork before she left to show some houses. She'd called the client that morning to see if they could meet at a nearby coffee shop. Dani planned to get her usual chai latte there. It wasn't a workable long-term strategy, avoiding the downstairs vendor in hopes that Bryce Grayson eventually transferred to Walla Walla, but it would get her through today.

By late afternoon, she'd hit her stride, happy with a number of new leads and feeling more herself than when she'd rolled out of bed. As predicted, Sonia Donavan phoned to discuss putting her house on the market. Although the woman was clearly bitter about her divorce, she had a razor-sharp sense of humor that had Dani biting her lip to stifle inappropriate laughter. She was grateful to find herself in a brighter mood leading up to dinner with her dad. She needed to convince him she wasn't brokenhearted over Tate.

Frankly, now that she'd had time and perspective to reevaluate her relationship, she was surprised her father had ever approved of the man. Next to her father, Tate Malcolm was such a small person. Literally and figuratively. Then again, it wasn't as if the two men had spent tons of time together.

"Um, Danica?"

Startled, she looked up from the unfinished email she was supposed to be typing. Great—it had taken her all day to assure Judy she was okay and now the receptionist caught her zoned out and staring into space. Oh, well. If the concerned woman brought some mini candy bars to cheer her up, Dani would just have to throw herself on the chocolate sword and eat a couple. It was the polite thing to do.

"What can I do for you, Judy?"

"Not for me." She lowered her voice to a whisper, her eyes the size of silver dollars. "For *him*. You'll never believe who's here to see you!" She dropped her voice again. By the time she added, "Hot Architect," Dani was lipreading.

Bryce Grayson had come to see her? Unlikely.

Sean.

Her heart thudded madly in her chest. She told herself it was an adrenaline surge caused by anger. There was absolutely no part of her that was eager to see him; she had more self-respect than that. More willpower. She couldn't undo Tate cheating on her or her stolen weekend with Sean, but she could learn from her mistakes. *No more liars for me.*

"Danica?" Judy prompted. "Do you want me to show him in?"

Hell, no. But dodging him felt cowardly. He was the one who should have difficulty facing her, not the other way around.

Clearing her throat, she straightened in her chair. "By all means."

Radiating unabashed curiosity over the visit, Judy ushered him into the office. It was definitely Sean, although he looked more like his brother than the last time she'd seen him. He wore a black polo shirt and khaki pants. He was clean shaven, and his hair was smoothed into a more conservative style. Still, those were superficial resemblances outweighed by glaring differences. She'd never confuse the two men again. Too bad she hadn't known Bryce was a twin on Saturday.

His gaze went straight to hers, the connection between them jolting. *Get over it*, she told her hormones. She warned her clients all the time not to be beguiled by an attractive exterior that could hide an alarming number of flaws. Sean Grayson was definitely not up to code.

She gestured toward the guest chairs on the other side of her desk. "Have a seat, *Gray*." She couldn't stop herself from sneering the nickname.

Judy gaped as if Dani had sprouted a second head— one with glowing red eyes and a skull covered in live snakes. The receptionist backed away slowly. "I, uh, was just headed home for the day, so…"

"Would you mind closing the door on your way out?" Dani requested in a gentler tone. Whatever Sean had to say, she didn't want anyone to overhear. Yet once the door was shut, she regretted her request. Being alone with him felt too intimate. Seconds scraped by in painful silence.

Instead of sitting, he rocked on the balls of his feet. "I wasn't trying to mislead you when I said my name was Gray. My friends really do call me that."

She would never use the nickname again. They weren't friends. "You want an honesty medal just because you didn't set out to mislead me?"

"What I want is to apologize. I understand if you don't forgive—"

"If?" She gripped the edge of her desk. "As in, you think there's a possibility I will? That just proves we jumped into bed too quickly. Because if you knew me at all, you'd understand how big a deal lying is." She didn't add that lying was only one of his crimes against her. The other, more humiliating one was how he'd made

her feel foolish for falling so fast. How many times had she admonished Meg to look before she leaped instead of giving her heart away casually?

Not that I gave him my heart! Sharing a sweaty, naked night with someone wasn't the same as falling in love. But she'd definitely been able to envision falling for him down the road. What had happened to her usual caution? The way he'd slipped past her defenses, effortlessly seducing her into lowering her guard, was unforgivable.

"This isn't actually a good time to talk," she said tightly. "I have a dinner date."

The muscles in his jaw visibly clenched. Was he bothered by the idea of her going out with another man, or did he think she was fibbing in order to get rid of him? *There's only one liar in this room.*

Whatever was running through his head, he tamped down his temper. In contrast to the blue fire in his eyes, his voice was pure courtesy. "Would there be a better time for us to talk?"

"I have a lot of showings this week," she evaded. "I'm surprised you even caught me in the office."

"It wasn't a coincidence. I saw your car in the lot when I drove by. And when I say drove by, I mean went three blocks out of my way to check if your car was here." He shoved a hand through his hair, making parts of it stand on end and eliminating some of the resemblance to his refined brother. "If I could go back and change things, Dani…"

She flinched. In the privacy of her apartment, his saying her name had been like a verbal caress. Now, it was insult on top of injury.

His gaze was a raw plea. "I can't stop thinking about you."

"Try. Very hard." She jerked her eyes away from his, refusing to be swayed. He looked genuinely sorry, but Tate had sounded sorry when he called to say he couldn't marry her, too. After-the-fact apologies were no reason to cave. Neither were mesmerizing blue eyes. Where was her self-discipline? She was the Major's daughter, a former basketball star who'd played an entire final quarter on a sprained ankle. "I don't want to see you again."

He sucked in a breath, his expression mutinous.

"Nothing you say is going to erase what happened," she interjected before he could speak. "And my father is meeting me here in a matter of minutes. You need to be gone before he arrives. He probably knows fifty ways to kill you with a paper clip." She picked one up off her desk and brandished it in warning.

"Worried about my safety?" Sean's lips twitched in a wan smile. "That must mean you care about me a little."

"I just don't want to risk blood in the carpet. My clients would find that off-putting."

Thinking she might evict him faster if she physically escorted him out, she rose and came around her desk. *Strategic fail.* She'd overestimated her immunity to his nearness. As she got closer, she noticed how good he smelled. She imagined she could feel the heat from his body. She certainly felt the heat in his gaze.

He stared at her, charged silence crackling around them. For a second, she thought he might be reckless enough to reach for her. What would she do if he tried to kiss her? The idea that he might be just that unpre-

dictable—or that, worse, her body might be traitorous
enough to respond—spurred her into action.

Giving him a wide berth, she hurried to the door,
breathing easier once it was open again. "You shouldn't
come back to this office unless you're selling a house.
Or buying one." She flashed a saccharine smile. "In
which case, I'd be happy to recommend one of my colleagues."

Shoulders slumped, he headed toward the doorway.
Seeing him dejected felt unnatural, like seeing a ma-
jestic wild animal caged. Errant compassion tried to
surface, but she squelched it.

He paused beside her, a sad half smile playing about
his lips. "You know, it's my birthday. At least I know
what to wish for."

He'd told her he was turning thirty-four today. With
all that had happened, she'd forgotten.

Standing this close to him, recalling what it felt like
to be in his arms, she couldn't help wishing things
were different, too. But she resolutely brushed away
the pointless what-ifs. "I don't back down, Mr. Grayson. No amount of wishing is going to change that."

"Probably not." He stepped out of her office, throwing her one last look over his shoulder, this one display-
ing more of his usual spark. "But stranger things have
happened."

Dani and her dad had a favorite Italian restaurant near
the Perimeter. The food was well worth the inevitable
traffic, but he picked her up at her office so they could at
least catch up while they sat sandwiched between semi-
trailers and frustrated moms in SUVs. Unfortunately,
that also gave them a lot of time alone without the dis-

traction of deciding what to order or enjoying their dinner. His chatter about a recent bowling tournament and a summer fishing trip he was planning with other retired Army buddies only took them so far. He kept turning the conversation back to her life, unappeased by her declarations of how much she loved her job.

"That's work, Danica Leigh. I want to know about *you*. Your personal life."

No, you really don't.

He switched lanes to get them closer to their approaching exit. "You don't look like you've been sleeping well." Trust the eagle-eyed Major to notice—and be blunt enough to comment on it. "The thought of you pining for that no-good... I know a West Point guy who went on to be CIA. I bet if I call in a few favors, we could have Malcom disappear."

She laughed. "Don't say things like that at the restaurant. If someone overhears, they may not realize you're joking."

Her father shot her a pointed look.

"Dad, I am not heartbroken over Tate Malcom. I wish him and the new missus health and happiness." Well, happiness might be a stretch. But she didn't wish that an anvil would fall on either of them anymore or that Tate would suddenly contract a rare wasting disease. "He wasn't right for me. Honestly, looking back, I'm a little surprised you liked him." Looking back, she was surprised *she'd* liked him.

But Tate was attractive and deceptively charming. They had similar backgrounds and compatible long-term goals, so in sync on the big issues that she'd overlooked seemingly trivial irritations. When you found a guy who whole-heartedly supported your career, shared your philosophies on life and knew what it was like to grow up with only one parent, how much should it matter that he got cranky when you wore high heels?

Her father was mulling over her statement about liking Tate. "He may not have been specifically who I would have chosen for you, but I trusted your judgment. You've always had a good head on your shoulders."

Heat rose in her cheeks as she recalled her wild weekend. Yeah, she was the epitome of careful judgment. She squirmed in the passenger seat, feeling as though she was sixteen again, on the verge of being busted.

"But if he wasn't the One, well, there are other fish in the sea," he added.

Dani rolled her eyes. "We've got 'good head on my shoulders' and 'other fish.' We just need 'where one door closes, another opens' for the cliché hat trick."

Her father grinned. "Smart-ass."

"I know there are other fish, but I don't think I'm interested in recasting anytime soon." She should take the advice she frequently gave Meg about not rushing headlong into anything. Her rash impulse to take Sean home with her had been a total mistake.

Really? Because it was the best night you've had in... All right, an enjoyable error in judgment, but an error all the same.

"You do still want to get married?" her dad pressed. "I'd hate to see you live your life alone just because Malcom's too dumb to know what he had."

"I haven't technically sworn off men for all time, but I'm in no hurry to race down the aisle."

He didn't respond, but he was scowling, which surprised her.

"Is this you being anxious to have grandchildren?" she asked. "Because you didn't bring me up to believe I needed a man."

"Of course you don't 'need' one. I just want you to be happy. Being alone is…" His eyes were fixed straight ahead, but she didn't get the impression he was looking at the cars in front of them.

"Dad, did you ever think about remarrying?" There had been a few girlfriends who'd drifted through their life, but as far as Dani could tell, none of those relationships had ever come close to getting serious.

"Not really. Your mom was my one great love. I want that for you, too. I guess I've been so worried about this Tate thing because I was afraid you were like me. That you might not experience true love twice." A surprisingly boyish smile creased his face. "When I met Gina, I was so over the moon for her. Couldn't eat, couldn't sleep, couldn't think straight."

"And this is what you want for me?" she asked drily. She was already lacking sleep and appetite, and her train of thought had fallen off the tracks multiple times today. It was not an enjoyable state.

"Well. The infatuation part fades into something deeper," her dad said. "Something everyone should have."

That definitely didn't describe what she'd had with Tate. *And Sean?* If he hadn't lied to her, would the all-consuming, gotta-have-you-now attraction between them have burned itself out or eventually evolved into something more? *Guess we'll never know.* For the first time since he'd walked out of her apartment yesterday morning, she felt a flicker of relief. After almost marrying the wrong man, she was skittish about getting seriously involved with anyone else, not ready to trust her judgment on anything more than a casual fling.

Whatever might have happened between her and Sean, it was impossible to imagine it being casual.

SEAN WAITED AS his friend fished a quarter out of his pocket so they could flip for break. The bar was pretty dead on a Tuesday night, so they'd had their pick of pool tables. Although, they could have just stayed upstairs and had a drink—Sean wasn't deluded enough to believe he'd be able to concentrate on the game.

"How'd you find this place?" Alex asked. "It's... quaint." He wasn't being condescending, only expressing genuine surprise. Like Sean, Alex Juarez was single. This was more the kind of neighborhood place they frequented when they were out with the married guys on the crew, instead of bars where women tended to be looking for company.

"A friend brought me here. I liked it." The real question was, what had drawn him back here tonight? Had he subconsciously wanted to relive the memory of shooting pool with Dani, or was he hoping to engineer an "accidental" run-in with her? *As if she wouldn't see through that lameness in about two seconds flat.*

Well, he'd failed with the direct approach at her office yesterday. And she'd already thrown him out of her apartment. He was running out of options. *This is sad, man. Keep it up and you'll be getting a restraining order as a belated birthday present.*

Alex flipped the coin, which landed on tails, leaving Sean the break. But his muscles tensed, and it was a crap shot, barely disrupting the balls.

"Hijole." Alex glanced at him with wide eyes, then

snickered. "What happened to the great Gray? My nine-year-old niece breaks better than that. No one on the crew's gonna believe me."

"Maybe you should have recorded a video on your phone," Sean grumbled, stepping aside.

"What's going on with you?" Alex tapped a pocket, took his shot and missed. "You're preoccupied. Like right there!"

Sean blinked. "Right what?"

"You were busy staring up there." Alex pointed past the railing toward the top half of the split-level bar. "Didn't even see me make my shot," he said slyly.

"Nice try," Sean countered. "You missed. Good aim. Not enough follow-through."

The other man shrugged. "Worth a try. What are you looking at, anyway? Hot girl? Did you bring me here because you're planning to make a move on one of the waitresses?"

"No." He couldn't even say with certainty whether the woman who'd brought them their drinks had been a blonde, a brunette or a redhead. He'd been too busy glancing toward the entrance, fingers mentally crossed.

"So what gives? You were distracted on the site today, too."

Distraction and power tools were a bad combination. Most of his duties these days were supervisory and administrative, but, still, his crew deserved better from him. He just needed to find a way to stop obsessing over Dani. She was like a splinter under his thumb he couldn't reach. Or a song stuck in his head. He fell asleep with the tune playing on a loop and woke up with it still there. It had been a long time since a woman had gotten to him like this.

Was his extreme reaction because of guilt? He recalled the way she'd moaned when he was inside her, the way she'd arched against him, unashamedly craving his touch. Nope, guilt was definitely not the only reason he couldn't stop thinking about her. "Ever have a woman you couldn't get off your mind?"

Alex stilled, his expression disbelieving. "Is this about that high-maintenance blonde you were dating?"

"Tara? Hell, no. She's out of my life for good." More or less. He'd see her in passing next weekend. She'd wheedled a favor out of him before they broke up, and since it was for a good cause, he'd decided to honor the obligation. But aside from their paths crossing that one last time, he doubted he'd run into her again. She spent about as much time in his favorite bars as he did buying designer clothes at Lenox Square. "I was talking about someone different."

Different was accurate on many levels. Dani's mannerisms were unlike many of the women he'd dated. No other one-night stand had ever affected him like this.

"So you're hung up on a new lady," Alex surmised. "Have you told her? Women dig that, makes you seem vulnerable. You could get very lucky."

"She knows." It was almost cringe-worthy, the way he'd opened up to her yesterday and been shot down. "And she's not interested."

Alex whistled. "Failing with women *and* at pool? Damn. Well, if she isn't interested, you know the saying. Best way to get over someone is under someone else."

Far from convincing him to seek out another woman's attention, the statement only reminded him of meeting Dani. *"My fiancé eloped last weekend with the woman he was seeing on the side... I need to have a really good time and forget the whole mess... Want to help generate a little amnesia?"* She'd been incredibly, disarmingly candid.

Too bad he hadn't returned the favor.

With that sour thought, he resolved to focus on the game. He could count on one hand the number of times Alex had beat him at pool, and he didn't intend to simply hand him another victory. Several turns later, when Alex lifted his cue a fraction too soon after a draw shot, Sean saw his opportunity to pull ahead. But then he heard a man upstairs call out, "Hey, Danny," and he knocked the cue ball off the table. When he turned around, he saw that the guy had been greeting another man. Not Danica.

Alex won the game handily, his grin mocking when he asked, "Play again?"

"Nah. We have an early morning."

"Plus, you can't play for crap tonight."

"That, too."

They paid their tab and headed for the exit. On the way out, a curvy redhead grinned in Sean's direction. He tried to muster an answering smile, but the effort was so weak Alex cocked an eyebrow at him.

"Whoever this new woman is," Alex said in the parking lot, "you must really be hung up on her."

"Seems like." The question was, how did he win her forgiveness? On the surface, Sean might not be as overtly successful as his brother, but the truth was, he simply cared about different things. When he set his mind to something, he was persistent. And nine times out of ten, he accomplished what he set out to do.

It's only been a couple of days. With a little patience

and luck, he'd figure out something. Granted, Dani was stubborn. But perhaps she'd met her match.

THE FIRST STREET in the Magnolia Groves subdivision was lined with luxurious new homes. Colorful flowers bloomed along front porches, and a trim woman in yoga pants pushed a stroller along the sidewalk. But as Dani turned onto the second street, manicured lawns gave way to red Georgia dirt, unfinished wooden structures and cement foundations. The pristine model home looked almost out of place amid the active construction.

In the lot next to the model home was a trailer sporting the building company logo. A familiar looking blonde was coming down the steps. Dani recognized her as Lydia Reynolds, who worked for another brokerage. The two women had done deals together before, but Lydia rarely concentrated on brand-new subdivisions. She was considered quite the expert on foreclosures.

Dani waved as Lydia approached. "Nice to see you."

Lydia air-kissed her. "Here to register clients? The builder's agent called in sick today, but the site supervisor gave me a walk-through of the prototype." She lowered her voice to a confidential whisper. "Between you and me, it was hard to concentrate on the features of the house instead of looking at him. *Nice.*"

Laughing, Dani told the other woman they should meet for drinks soon. *Just not at the bar near my place.* It was going to be a long while before Dani could go in there without remembering her night with Sean, which was neither fair nor logical. She'd been to that bar dozens of times. Why should an isolated night stand out more starkly than any of the instances that had come before it?

As Lydia climbed into her car, Dani strode toward the trailer, her newest pair of open-toed pumps clicking on the sidewalk. She'd bought them yesterday; the buckles at the ankle and studs on the T-strap made her feel like a bad-ass. In her mind, she wore them with black jeans, a leather jacket and a shirt that said "Mess with Me at Your Peril" instead of a fitted jersey dress. "Danica?"

She whipped her head around, sure she must be imagining his voice. Maybe it was another real-estate agent she knew, one who happened to sound like Sean. But, no, there he was. In the flesh. He was right behind her, at the bottom of the trailer stairs.

It took her a moment to find her voice. "Wh-what are you doing here?" But she'd already noticed the logo on the chambray button-down he wore with the sleeves rolled up.

"I work here." A smile spread across his face. "I'm the lead builder for Magnolia Grove."

She blinked, her thoughts a chaotic jumble. At least now she knew what he did for a living.

8

DANI'S TONGUE SEEMED stuck to the roof of her mouth. *Be a professional. You've dealt with builders before.* Dealt with, yes. Slept with, no.

"I, uh… The Andersens." She was relieved she remembered the name of the couple interested in upgrading to a larger house. "I wanted to take a look around and, if the neighborhood meets their criteria, schedule a showing."

"Absolutely." He crossed his arms across his chest, and she was annoyed that her gaze went to the tanned muscles displayed. "I realize I'm biased, but Magnolia Grove is shaping up to be a very nice place to live. You look fantastic."

The compliment caught her off guard. It was difficult to remind herself that their exchange was strictly professional when his expression was so personal.

He gestured toward the trailer door. "After you."

Considering the temptation of being alone with him in her office Monday, going into the trailer now seemed like a bad idea. "I think I'd rather do a walk-through of the house."

He smirked but said nothing as he retreated down the steps. The sunlight glinted off his hair, highlighting a few golden strands, and she cursed the general unfairness of the universe. As tough as it had been to resist him on Monday while staring into those earnest blue eyes, she'd risen to the challenge. Test passed, level cleared. She was free to move forward.

Yet here he was again.

You withstood his charm last time, you will again. It would only get easier with time, right?

Could he see her tension, her rigid posture as she matched his stride? He opened the front door of the model home, and a static charge ran down her body as she passed him.

She took a deep breath, willing herself to relax. It didn't work. *Maybe I should join Meg for one of those yoga classes she's always trying to drag me to.* A list of standard questions ran through her head, their familiarity comforting. This wouldn't be like the awkward confrontation in her office. She didn't have to flounder with what to say; she had a script. Fighting for composure, she turned to face him.

His mouth was curled into a satisfied grin that made him look entirely too smug. *And sexy.*

She huffed out a breath. "What?"

"I was just taking a moment to thank her."

Oh, fun. Mind games. "Her, who?"

His grin widened, humor gleaming in his eyes. "The fairy godmother *I* obviously have, since here you are."

"Guys don't get fairy godmothers. It isn't manly."

"Sexist."

"I'm here to talk about the subdivision," she said. "Not us."

"At least you're acknowledging the possibility of us. That's progress."

"No, I—"

"So this is a six-bedroom house," he began, walking from the foyer toward the back of the house, leaving her little choice but to follow. "Three and a half baths."

"Actually, would you mind if I look around by myself for a little bit and make some notes? Then I'll have a better idea of what I want from you. I mean," she amended quickly, "what questions I want to ask."

"Sure." His smiling, self-assured air faded into something more solemn but no less alluring. "If you need some time and space, I can give you that. But you know where to find me when you're ready."

FOR THE MOST PART, Dani felt as if she left Magnolia Grove with her dignity intact. When she'd finished her cursory inspection of the house and asked Sean a couple of questions about amenities, she'd sounded poised. Hopefully, he would accept that she'd put their passionate night behind her.

It would be nice if at least one of them could believe she had.

Truthfully, seeing him had unbalanced her. Work was her sanctuary. The last thing she'd expected was to interact with him on the job. It left her vaguely off-kilter for the next couple of hours.

When she joined Spencer and Judy for lunch in one of their meeting rooms, she kept losing her place in the conversation, her thoughts reverting to Sean. How was it fair that he looked equally sexy when he was being playful or sincere? And she felt as though she'd seen him in his element now. He'd spoken about the subdivision with genuine pride. It was obvious he cared about his work as much as she did hers.

"Danica?" Spencer's tone was quizzical. "Don't you have a closing today?"

Her gaze shot to the clock on the wall. "Oh, *hell*. That's the time already?" It was still theoretically possible that she wouldn't be late, but she liked to allow plenty of time for unpredictable traffic.

Moving like a whirling dervish, she cleaned up her fast-food debris, gathered some files from her office, hoisted her purse onto her shoulder and darted through the reception area. At the far end of the hallway, the elevator doors were starting to slide closed.

"Hold the elevator, please!" She liked her strappy pumps slightly less at the moment—they weren't optimal for jogging. But, check mark in the lucky column, someone in the elevator had heard her. The doors reversed direction. And she found herself face-to-face with Bryce Grayson.

She smothered a groan.

His eyes widened. "You." He took a reflexive step farther away, looking even less eager to be in her presence than he had the morning she'd almost caused him to spill his coffee. At the moment, he didn't really live up to his moniker. He was more Wary Architect.

"I'm guessing your brother mentioned me, then?" She glanced at the ceiling, wishing she'd ignored the opportunity to jump on the elevator and had stuck to her usual custom of taking the stairs. How much had Sean revealed? Did Bryce know that she'd slept with his brother believing it was him?

"Yes, he did." He cleared his throat. "Skimmed over

the details, but I, uh, got the idea. I was shocked—no one ever confuses the two of us."

Because her mistake was somehow more shocking than a guy seducing her under a false identity? "Well, you are identical." Sort of. "I mean, until someone gets to know you."

"But you and I *don't* know each other. So why would you believe…" He paused, looking as if he found this entire exchange distasteful. "Have I ever done anything that would lead you to think—"

Ding.

Oh, thank the sweet Lord. They'd reached the ground floor.

"I don't make a habit of going home with women I don't know," he blurted as the doors parted.

She was torn between wanting to defend herself—explaining that it had been atypical behavior for her, too—and vehemently telling herself she didn't owe the judgmental guy any explanation at all.

Since she was already running late, she limited her reply to a tight smile and a clipped, "You have a nice day." But as she turned toward the parking lot, she couldn't refrain from asking, "You are just twins, right? Not triplets or anything?"

His forehead crinkled in a frown. "Right."

"Good." She'd hit her quota on Grayson brothers for the day. Two was bad enough. Having to deal with a third would be enough to drive a girl to a psychotic break.

BEMUSED, BRYCE GRAYSON watched as the brunette bolted across the parking lot. His own vehicle was in the opposite direction, and he was due for a late lunch downtown.

As he started his car, he pondered Danica Yates; he'd made it a point to find out her last name after Sean shared his sordid tale. The real-estate agent was a far cry from Sean's last lover, the bubbly blonde who was involved with several good causes. Bryce had seen her at one or two charity events. He didn't know what to make of Danica, but she was not bubbly.

She'd seemed nice enough the few times their paths had crossed, but he couldn't imagine what he'd said or done that would have made her think he was trying to get her into bed. Bryce was appalled by his brother's actions. And since Sean had seduced her in *his* name, he couldn't help feeling a sense of responsibility. If he'd led Ms. Yates on, if he'd somehow had a hand in making his brother's lie believable…

When she'd stepped onto the elevator, he hadn't known what to do. He'd felt an irrational need to apologize. It grated, after so many years of trying to do the right thing, that he would find himself having to say he was sorry on behalf of his brother. Let Sean clean up his own messes.

He wondered if Ms. Yates's sharp-tongued responses were misplaced anger. Maybe she was taking out her frustration with Sean on Bryce since they looked alike. Bryce had no idea how to appease her, and not knowing how to proceed made him awkward. One of the reasons he was so good at his detail-oriented job was that he preferred clear cut policies that outlined exactly what to do. Trying to figure out what to say to Ms. Yates had knotted his stomach.

Judging by the way she'd stalked off, the conversation had been no more pleasant on her end.

Given how far out of his depth he was in this social situation, maybe he should start coming to work a few minutes earlier and leaving later. Avoiding her was manageable. The question of his brother, however, was more irksome. Buried among memories of Sean's thoughtlessness were also recollections of friendship. They'd been close once.

By the time Bryce had finished unwrapping that art print Sean had commissioned for his birthday, he'd had a lump in his throat. But when he'd picked up the phone to thank his twin, he'd been immobilized by his brother's words. *You think about yourself enough for the both of us.*

Part of Bryce mourned the loss of their boyhood friendship. But they were men now. If he weren't related to Sean and happened to meet him as an adult, was there any logical basis for friendship? As far as he could tell, they didn't have a damn thing in common.

DANI PULLED INTO the shaded parking lot, amazed that the capricious gods of Atlanta traffic had bestowed their favor on her. *And I didn't even have to sacrifice a virgin or slay a Gorgon.* She arrived at the attorney's office with time to spare.

Erik's office suite was on the third floor, and his secretary nodded a friendly hello when Dani stepped inside.

"He's in conference room two," the secretary said. "I'll send the Kenners back when they arrive. And nice shoes!"

"Thanks." Dani grinned. "Yesterday's impulse buy."

Well, semi impulsive. She'd worn out her last pair of favorite black pumps, and she'd had an online coupon for
that particular shoe store. Spur-of-the-moment wasn't
her typical style. Coming on to Sean Grayson had been
an anomaly.

Even then, there had been extenuating circumstances
and she never would have done it if she hadn't already
been somewhat attracted to Bryce. Based on his half-
finished question in the elevator, when he'd wondered
what he'd done to make her think he was interested,
that attraction had clearly been one-sided. The funny
thing was, having seen Sean and Bryce in the same
day, it was hard to pinpoint why she'd found Bryce so
attractive in the first place. Now, he seemed like a pale
imitation of his brother. Sean was—

Off-limits. Remember?

Banishing him from her thoughts, she entered the
conference room.

"Danica." Erik stepped forward to shake her hand,
his smile warm. "Would you like something to drink?"
A pitcher of water sat on a small counter to the side
of the wide mahogany table, and a pot of coffee was
plugged into the wall.

"Water would be great, thanks."

He poured her a glass, but when he handed it to her,
a flash of apprehension crossed his gaze.

"Is everything okay?" she asked. There shouldn't
be any last-minute surprises at closing. She glanced
toward the papers on the table. "If there's some kind
of problem—"

"No, no problem."

"Oh. Sorry. I thought you looked…nervous."

"Did I?" He rubbed a hand across his jaw. "Guess it's been a while since I asked a woman out."

Her mouth dropped open. "You wanted to ask me out?"

"It doesn't have to be a date in the romantic sense," he said quickly. "My sister's on the committee for an upcoming benefit, and she talked me into buying a couple of tickets. It's to raise money for a group that provides summer meals for kids who qualify for free meals during the school year but are left with a two- to three-month nutritional gap. Anyway. There's a summer-themed fashion show and dinner at the country club two Saturdays from now." He was trying to keep his tone casual, but there was a hint of vulnerability in his gaze.

She knew what it was like to put yourself out there, recalling the excruciating moment on Saturday when she'd assumed Sean's pause was a precursor for telling her no. Had he been trying to decide how to tell her she had the wrong guy?

"Erik, I appreciate the invitation, but you and I work together quite a bit. Dating someone who's a part of my professional life could be…" She relived the shock she'd felt when Sean walked around the corner of the model home this morning. It had hit her with nearly physical force.

"I understand. But I do still have that extra ticket." He smiled sheepishly. "And Margot's going to be there with her new boyfriend. I'd much rather take a friend than show up alone."

"Ah." The catch in his voice when he said his ex-wife's name was unmistakable. Maybe the reason he lacked practice asking out women was because he hadn't yet gotten over Margot. "In that case, let me check my schedule and get back to you. If I'm free, I'd love to go. As a friend."

Schedule permitting, she'd be happy to help him out. He was funny and articulate and well liked. Best of all, he wasn't a Grayson.

9

THE ANDERSENS WERE some of Dani's favorite clients. Several years ago, she'd helped them buy a house when they were the brand-new parents of a baby girl. Now they were expecting twins and ready to upgrade. The Magnolia Grove subdivision, which managed to blend high-end amenities with a burgeoning close-knit community feel, seemed right in their wheelhouse.

Dread filled her as she drove through the redbrick entrance to the neighborhood. "Well, here we are."

"Um…" From the passenger seat, Natalie Andersen slanted her a quizzical look. "Is there something we should know about this subdivision? I've heard your enthusiastic voice before, and that wasn't it."

"Sorry, I was thinking about something else. Momentary aberration." Dani could have kicked herself for the lapse in professionalism. Whether they ran into Sean today or not, her clients deserved her full attention. "This neighborhood has a lot of potential. Control is in the transition phase between the building company and eventual homeowner's association. People who move in now can help steer the direction of HOA governance."

She parked in front of the model home, trying to keep her gaze from darting toward the trailer. She failed. Almost as if he'd been watching for her—or as if fate were conspiring against her—the door opened and Sean stepped out with a man in a hard hat. The other man nodded at something, then departed in the opposite direction. Sean, however, smiled at Dani as she climbed out of her car and headed in his direction.

His grin was full of mischief as he called out, "If it isn't my favorite fairy god-agent."

Bippity boppity bite me.

"Good to see you, Danica."

She gave him a bland smile. "This is Natalie and Ross Andersen."

"Nice to meet you. Sean Grayson." He shook hands with both of them. "Danica's already familiar with the display home, but if you don't mind my horning in for a few minutes, I can point out a few things that can be customized and what variations we offer on the floor plan."

The Andersens seemed happy to have his input. He was using her clients as human shields, knowing Dani couldn't kick him to the curb while maintaining her professional veneer. Behind Natalie's back, Dani scowled at him in silent accusation.

He responded with a beatific smile.

They proceeded through a generous foyer into the living room. Although the house was a two-story, the upstairs rooms were built around the first floor in an L-shape. The living room had a high ceiling with two skylights.

Natalie smiled up at them, charmed. "I wonder if you can see any stars at night."

"Doubtful." Ross joined his wife beneath a skylight, putting an arm around her waist. "They've done a nice job of preserving trees around here and not putting the houses right on top of each other, but it's still an urban area. All the light pollution washes out the night sky."

"Oh, I don't know," Sean said softly, for Dani's ears only. "I've certainly seen stars in a living room."

Sense memories blazed through her. Their mingled cries in her own living room. The leather of the couch cool against her skin, contrasting with the trail of heat created by his hands. She tried not to think about how closely he'd held her afterward.

Sean pivoted on his heel. "And right through here is the kitchen." The model home included a flat-top stove and a kitchen island. "These counters are standard height, but we've also done some customization in the neighborhood to make individual kitchens more ergonomic."

"Deviating from the norm can hurt resale value," Dani warned her clients.

"One compromise for that is altering the height of a single counter surface to give yourself a break," Sean suggested. "After all, people spend a lot of time in the kitchen. Standing, stretching to reach things, bending over…"

His gaze flickered to Dani, and her cheeks flamed. At the earliest opportunity, she was going to replace that damn couch.

His voice was completely composed as he continued talking about the kitchen, not betraying any sign that he shared her mental images. As he led them through the bedrooms, his demeanor was friendly but business-like. Few listening would ever realize he was simultaneously having two different conversations—one with the Andersens, and one with her. Whatever assurances she'd made herself that she could remain strictly professional, he wasn't playing by the same rules.

He showed them the master bathroom, with its spacious tiled shower and built-in bench. "I wish the shower in my town house was this roomy," he joked. "Heck, you could fit two people in here. Easily."

For a moment, she could almost feel steam caressing her body as Sean lathered shampoo through her hair. She gave herself a mental shake, pulling herself out of the memory, glad neither of the Andersens seemed to notice. But Sean's eyes met hers over the top of Natalie's head, his expression knowing.

After a quick scan of the bedroom and its vast walk-in closet, Natalie slid open the glass door that led to the balcony and stepped outside to check the view. "Ross, look. You can see how the entire neighborhood is laid out from up here."

He joined his wife, closing the door behind him.

The second they were alone, Dani socked Sean in the arm.

His lips quirked. "I'm not typically into the rough stuff. But for you, I—"

"What is *wrong* with you?" she demanded in a fierce whisper. If he pretended not to know what she was talking about, she was going to sock him again. "Do you normally try to seduce everyone that sets foot into the display home?"

"No. Just you."

The simple, poignant admission deflated her righteous fury. She'd expected him to play dumb and had been working herself up for a fight. Or, considering that the Andersens could rejoin them at any moment, at least a *really* angry glare. But he wasn't denying his actions.

Instead, he stared at her with such open hunger that if he pulled her into his arms right then, she wouldn't have been surprised. Indignant, maybe. Conflicted and confused and uncomfortably aroused. But not surprised.

"Sean…" Damn. The way she'd said his name didn't sound like the admonishment she'd intended. It sounded dangerously close to an invitation.

He reached out, his hand cupping the side of her face. She swayed on her feet, unconsciously leaning toward him. Desire warred with common sense. The Andersens were right outside.

"I screwed up." Compared to the amiable sales-pitch tone he'd been using, his voice seemed naked now, stripped of everything but unvarnished emotion. "I know how badly I screwed up. But if you'll give me a chance…"

Wasn't that what all liars and cheaters said? *It'll never happen again, baby. It was just this once.* Sean sounded more convincing than most, but that wasn't a guarantee. It might simply mean he was a skilled liar.

Seeming frustrated by her silence, he dropped his hand to his side. "You can't tell me you don't have any feelings about us."

"Buyer's remorse." She took a step back, crossing her arms over her chest. "And embarrassment. I shared a really uncomfortable elevator ride with your brother."

He winced. "You talked to Bryce?"

"Yeah. And, not that he's entitled to an opinion, but I don't think he approves of our jumping into bed together."

Sean's face tightened. "If he said one insulting word to you, I—"

"No, nothing outright." She was startled by his protective tone and how quickly he sprang to her defense. As an only child, she didn't have any personal basis for comparison when it came to sibling relationships, but she'd watched Meg with her family plenty of times. The Raffertys razzed each other and even seriously disagreed on occasion, but the core of their relationship was loyalty. They presented a united front to outsiders.

Apparently, such was not the case with Sean and his brother. One would think that identical twins, sharing the same DNA, would be the closest siblings of all.

"It wasn't that he said anything hateful," she clarified. "He just seems…"

"To have a stick up his butt?" He scrubbed a hand over his face. "Sorry. I shouldn't be crass. Or involve you in family squabbles. It's just that my holier-than-thou brother—"

"It is beautiful out there," Natalie said, stepping back inside. "Of course, if we moved into the neighborhood, I'd want a house *without* a view of the community pool. I'm not sure my self-esteem could take Ross watching babes in bikinis while I'm pregnant out to here with twins."

"Hey," her husband said sternly. "You *are* a babe. And carrying our children—" The unexpected sound of a foghorn filled the room. Ross pulled a cell phone from his pocket. "That's my agent. I need to take this." He retreated back onto the balcony for privacy.

"Twins, huh?" Sean smiled at Natalie. "I have a twin brother myself. We're nothing alike, though. He's Mr. Book Smart and I have what one counselor called 'kinesthetic intelligence.' Which is a fancy way of saying, I'm good with my hands."

Dani kept her gaze steadfastly locked on the base-board, refusing to risk a glance in his direction.

"We're having twin girls," Natalie said.

"Congratulations." Sean leaned forward, his voice an exaggerated whisper. "Boys are obnoxious handfuls."

Natalie laughed, while Dani resisted the urge to nod in emphatic agreement. Sean was infuriatingly, blood-pressure-raisingly obnoxious. But he was also so much more than that.

"How long have the two of you been married?" Sean asked conversationally.

"Seven years."

"Well, it's easy to see you were made for each other." Sean unknowingly echoed the opinion Dani had always held about the Andersens.

Natalie giggled. "It's sweet of you to say that, but it wasn't always apparent. We had a rather, er, tumultuous courtship."

The door behind them slid open, and Ross raised his eyebrows at his wife's amused expression. "Did I miss something funny?"

"Natalie was just telling us that, early on, the two of you hit some bumps in the road," Dani said. "Which, personally, I find impossible to believe."

"Oh, believe it. Although, calling them 'bumps' is kinder than I deserve." Ross grimaced, putting his arm around Natalie's shoulders. "Thank God my wife is a forgiving woman."

She snuggled against him. "You were worth forgiving. Besides, what choice did I have? My only other option was being without you."

The words reverberated through Dani. Even without turning her head, she could feel Sean's gaze on her, his silent entreaty. He wanted her to forgive him. And, frankly, it was tempting. Sean was the most exhilarating man she'd ever known.

But what was the saying? *Fool me once, shame on you...* Did she want to risk setting herself up to be made a fool of again? In Dani's opinion, the key part of Natalie's story wasn't that she'd forgiven her husband. It was her certainty that he'd been worth it.

Dani was nowhere near the neighborhood of certainty. That neighborhood hadn't even been zoned for development yet. Was Sean worth second-guessing herself, going back on what she felt was a wise decision? There was one absolute way to know for sure, but she didn't think she could face the consequences of being wrong.

AFTER WORK FRIDAY, Dani attended an orientation meeting for all the volunteers in the softball league, then grabbed a late dinner with a few of the other coaches. It was almost ten when she got home, and it had been a fairly eventful week. She took a quick shower, planning to curl up with a good book afterward. She deserved some downtime.

But once she'd shimmied into a pair of comfortable pajamas and scanned both her e-reader and bedroom shelf for choices, she realized she felt too manic to concentrate. Restless and edgy. *That would be the sexual frustration.*

She rejected the thought as soon as it crossed her mind. Frustrated, because of a few paltry moments alone with Sean today? Ha! She'd been celibate for *months* and had survived just fine. She was not going to become a needy hostage to her hormones. For crying out loud, it had only been a week since she'd had sex.

Really, really great sex.

A knock sounded at her front door. Dani was so tightly strung that she jumped. Who the hell was showing up unannounced at this hour of the night? *Sean.*

The unbidden thought made her go liquid inside. There'd been that moment today when he'd considered going for broke and kissing her—she'd seen it in his eyes, heard it in the change of his breathing. If he was rash enough to do it, did she trust herself not to kiss him back? No.

She was honest enough to admit to herself that, if she opened the door and let him in, they were going to make love. She just didn't know if that's what she wanted.

Another knock interrupted her mental debate. *Down, girl. It's probably not even him.* One of her neighbors had given Dani a spare key for the times she'd locked herself out of her apartment, which was four and counting. Dani went into her living room warily, as if Sean's magnetism might be too much for her to resist even through metal-reinforced wood.

"Who is it?" she called, not yet close enough to look through the peep-hole.

"It's me." Muffled sniffling came from the other side. "Meg."

Dani unfastened the chain and turned the deadbolt. "You're the last person I expected to see." She knew from their chats earlier this week that Meg and Nolan had special plans tonight. It was their six-month anniversary.

"Sorry I didn't call first," Meg said. "I left the house in such a hurry I forgot that my phone was on the charger instead of in my purse."

"You know you're always welcome, any time day

or night. No advance notice require." She ushered her inside, getting a clearer look at her friend. Something was obviously wrong.

Meg wore a slinky green dress and killer gold sandals. At some point, she'd also been wearing suitably dramatic evening makeup. But mascara that had no doubt started the evening on her lashes now formed rivulets over blotchy red cheeks. Meg sniffed, and Dani turned to find her a box of tissues.

"Here."

Meg took the box but hardly seemed to register what it was for. She clutched it against her, staggering numbly toward the sofa, offering no clue what was wrong.

Dani took a stab in the dark. "Don't tell me he forgot your anniversary."

"No, he asked me to marry him."

And that warranted sobbing? Dani blinked, trying to connect the dots between a proposal and her friend's current condition. "Are these…happy tears?" They sure as hell didn't look like it.

Meg made a loud, honking sound midway between a laugh and a sob. "Hardly! Before I could even think how to answer him, he was outlining our future. You know how he's a little older than you and me? Well, it turns out he's in quite a hurry to become a father."

"And this was the first you'd heard about it?"

"I knew he wanted to be a dad someday. I didn't know he wanted to be one *now.* I have nieces and nephews. I love them, but I see how much work they are. There are a lot of things a childless married couple can do that they might not have the freedom—or disposable income—for after kids come along. When I tried telling Nolan that, it was like he misunderstood, that he just thought I was worried I wouldn't be a good mom, so he kept reassuring me and trying to get me to see things his way."

Recalling how Meg had come to her rescue post-Sean with mimosas, Dani asked, "Do we need liquor for this?" She wasn't sure what she had in the cabinets, but if it would help her friend, she'd find something.

Meg blew her nose. "Can I just have some ice water? I'm feeling a little dehydrated."

"Coming right up." She filled two glasses and returned to the living room. "For what it's worth, when you decide you are ready for children—many moons from now—you will make a fantastic mom."

Her friend had an innately nurturing spirit and optimistic outlook. She was fun, the kind of mother who would finger-paint with her kids and laugh at the mess, but she was also a successful businesswoman, smart and savvy. And unlike Dani, she'd never accidentally swear in front of young ears.

Meg gave her a watery smile, showing appreciation for the support. "If Nolan had said anything like that, I might still be there now. His repeated attempts to bring me around to his way of thinking are what caused the excrement to really hit the fan. He told me he'd known from the first time he laid eyes on me that I was made to be a mom, that I had a generous smile and compassionate eyes. And child-bearing hips."

Dani choked on her water.

"Yeah. I took offense, too, but he assured me it was a compliment, not criticism, that he considers me 'pleasingly plump.'"

"He called you *plump*? Bastard."

"It was so awful. Here was this guy offering me

everything I want, but he ruined it. He kept saying he loves me, but I'm not sure he understands me at all. Get this—in the imaginary future he has all mapped out for us, he assumed I'd quit working at the store to be a stay-at-home mom. He said that remaining a silent partner would bring welcome income, but that selling corsets and lace panties isn't a respectable job for a mother. Tell that to my sister who co-owns the place and has two kids!"

"I'd pay money to see him tell your sister. Marissa would lay him out flat."

"The more he talked, the clearer it became that I've completely wasted the past six months. And it's not like I can keep living in his house now that I've broken up with him. Can I stay here tonight?"

"Of course." The sofa folded out into a bed. "Not the poshest of accommodations, but *mi* crappy apartment *es su* crappy apartment. Seriously, stay as long as you need." As a real-estate agent, she knew there were dozens of factors that played into choosing a living arrangement. Desperation shouldn't be one of them. There was no need for Meg to go from one rash housing situation to another. "For now, all we have to do is address getting your stuff out of Nolan's place and into temporary storage. The rest, we'll figure out with time."

Meg's face crumpled. "You were right all along. I never should have moved in with him so soon. Then I wouldn't be in this mess."

"Don't beat yourself up." Dani squeezed her shoulder. "It doesn't matter what I thought. You were brave enough to take a chance. I've been thinking a lot about chances." Second chances, missed chances. "They offer rewards and pose risks. How are we supposed to know which risks are worth it if we never take them?"

"Thank you." Meg leaned her head back, staring forlornly at the ceiling. "But for the record? I wish I hadn't taken it."

DUSK WAS FALLING across Decatur as Sean drove to his parents' on Sunday evening. His mom had called earlier in the week, insisting that both her sons come over for a belated birthday celebration and see the pictures from Hawaii.

"I managed to get them loaded onto my computer," Keely Grayson had said proudly. "All four hundred and thirty-three! Bryce says there's something he can do so that we can watch them on the TV. Like an old-fashioned slide show."

Four hundred photos seemed a bit extreme to Sean. Still, he was looking forward to the Never-Ending Slide Show more than he was looking forward to seeing Bryce. For once, Sean would welcome one of his brother's last-minute cancellations. Keely hated it when her sons fought, but Sean wasn't sure how they could be in the same room without that happening. When he thought about how Bryce had made Dani feel, his temper bubbled and boiled like one of the active volcanoes his parents had just visited.

Even though Dani had backpedaled, saying Bryce didn't technically insult her, when she'd mentioned the "uncomfortable elevator ride" and his implied disapproval, there'd been an expression on her face that veered dangerously close to shame. It was one thing for Bryce to occasionally hint that Sean was inferior. A degree of sibling rivalry was natural. But the idea of Bryce, of *anyone*, making Dani feel bad about herself? Sean's gut tightened in a knot of protectiveness and anger.

As he flipped on his blinker and moved into the turning lane to make a left onto his parents' street, he realized the luxury sedan in the opposite lane belonged to his brother. Sean suddenly found himself anxious to turn. If he got a moment alone with Bryce, he had a few opinions he could get off his chest before they had to make nice in front of their parents.

But there was a steady stream of oncoming traffic. Watching his brother's car make its way to the cul-de-sac, Sean knew he wouldn't have a chance to catch up with him. Goosing the accelerator and speeding down the residential street would earn his folks' dismay and snide remarks from Bryce.

By the time Sean parked in the driveway, his mom had already thrown open the door to greet Bryce on the wide wooden porch. The paint was peeling badly. Sean would have to check his schedule to see when he could apply a new coat.

He and Bryce had inherited their build from their father, a big, blond bear of a man, but they had their mother's coloring. Keely Grayson shared their light eyes and dark hair, although hers was liberally streaked with shining silver. She was a cheerful, vivacious woman, but she worried about her boys. Nothing made her tense up faster than the suggestion that something might be wrong in their lives. She also despaired of getting either of them married off, what with Bryce's "workaholic bent" and Sean's "skirt-chasing ways."

Lately, there was only one skirt he wanted to chase. As he climbed out of the SUV, he thought that his mom would probably be cheered by the news that Sean was interested in someone specific. But he couldn't figure out how to mention Dani without the story rapidly devolving into the type of anecdote you didn't confide to your parents.

"Sean!" She waved from the front porch. "Both my boys here at once. This is what I call a good day."

"And all those days you spent in sunny Hawaii?" Bryce teased without looking in his brother's direction. "They were what—slow grueling torture?"

She chuckled. "You know what I mean."

Bryce hoisted the box of imported bottled beer he carried. "I should put these in the fridge and say hi to dad."

"He's out back, getting the grill ready. See if he needs any help."

With an obedient nod, Bryce disappeared into the house.

Sean loped up the stairs and hugged his mom. "Welcome back, world traveler."

"You been behaving yourself since I saw you last?" she asked.

He grinned. "No, ma'am." It occurred to him that Bryce had probably never once been asked if he was behaving himself.

"Before you go inside, you should know that your dad is probably going to ask your opinion on some home improvement projects. If you love me, you'll discourage him. I swear, ever since he retired, when he gets bored, he knocks down a wall and I end up living with plaster and plastic sheets all over my house. He needs some other hobbies," she grumbled.

"Could be worse. He could spend his days hanging out at strip clubs."

She harrumphed, but her eyes were twinkling. "At least then I'd get some peace and quiet around here."

They entered the house together, and Sean knew from the cinnamon-spiced scent that his mom had been baking. He resisted the urge to close his eyes and revel in the aroma that, to him, equaled home. "Apple pie?"

"Your favorite. And French silk for your brother."

In the Grayson household, the tradition was birthday pies, not birthday cakes. Maybe if he'd made his birthday wish blowing out a candle on homemade pie, it would have come true and Dani would be speaking to him again. There were moments when he glimpsed encouraging signs of progress—the way she'd sighed his name and leaned toward him in the model home two days ago   but those tiny moments hadn't been enough to change the big picture.

He ducked into the kitchen, grabbing one of his dad's flip-top beers from the fridge. "Hey, Mom, has Dad ever seriously screwed up? Romantically, I mean?"

She put her hands on her hips. "The year he got me that steam mop for Valentine's Day comes to mind. Of course he's messed up, honey. We both have. We're only human. What's this about?"

"I…" The words *there's this girl* hovered on the tip of his tongue, and he suddenly felt as if he was eleven years old, having an afternoon snack and telling his mom about the cute brunette who won the fifth-grade spelling bee. She'd been out of his league, though. He'd never made above a B minus in spelling. "Never mind."

She studied him shrewdly. "Any time you mess up, a heartfelt apology is a good start."

"Without admitting to anything, let's assume I already tried that."

"Really?" She looked startled by that information. He supposed he did have a track record of being stubborn. "Well, flowers are—"

"Mom?" Bryce came in through the screen door at the back of the house. "Dad has questions for you about how long he's supposed to cook your salmon."

"Oh, for heaven's sake," she muttered. "I already went over this with him. Any time you give that man something to throw on the grill besides a burger or a steak, he gets as flustered as if you asked him to prepare a Baked Alaska. I'll be right back."

With his mom out of earshot, Sean wasted no time. "I understand you talked to Danica."

Bryce took a swig of his beer. "She told you that? I didn't realize the two of you were on speaking terms."

"We're… That's beside the point. Whether she's speaking to me or not, she deserves your respect."

"*I* disrespected her?" Bryce asked indignantly. "Oh, that's rich, coming from you. I don't know her well enough to feel anything for her, except sympathy that she got mixed up with you in the first place."

Sean ground his teeth, unpleasantly reminded that she'd only been "mixed up with" him by accident. He wasn't the brother she'd wanted. Of course, maybe if she'd known Bryce better and realized how pompous he could be…

"Honestly, I don't know why she'd care about my opinion, anyway," Bryce said. "She didn't seem to like me very much."

Hearing that qualified as the high point of Sean's day.

"On the other hand." Bryce gestured with his bottle.

"She didn't seem to like *you* very much, either. Made a crack about how she was glad there weren't any more of us."

"She's upset. Understandably. But I'm working on that."

Bryce stared at him for a long moment. "You're serious, aren't you?"

"Yeah."

"But I meant what I said about her not liking you. You've never had a problem getting dates. Why are you pursuing her? You should—"

"What, just give up?" Great brotherly advice—tell the loser to cut his losses.

To hell with this. Sean decided to see if his dad could use his help.

But as he left the room, he glanced back at Bryce. "It may surprise you to hear this, but I *do* succeed at some things." He just didn't know yet whether persuading Dani to give him a second chance would be one of them.

_10_

DANI WAS WRITING up new listings Thursday midmorning when her cell phone rang. She checked the screen. Meg.

"Hey." She leaned back in her chair. "I was going to call you later. Do you have any lunch plans? The couple I was showing houses to canceled, so I have an unexpected, sinfully indolent gap in the middle of my day."

There was a pause on Meg's end. "Thanks for the offer, but I have a lot to do here at the store. We're transitioning from spring stock to summer."

Dani bit her lip to keep from laughing. She knew people often put away sundresses for the winter or shoved boxes of sweatshirts under their beds once summer rolled around, but she hadn't realized there was a difference between spring and summer undies. "Are summer thongs more revealing than the spring ones?"

"Watch it," Meg threatened. "Your friends-and-family discount isn't carved in stone, you know. Respect the thongs."

Not likely. But since she did respect her friend's business enterprise—and because it was fun to occasionally slip into something uncharacteristically frilly—she didn't point out that before meeting Meg, she'd been perfectly content buying basic undergarments at retail chains.

"If you're really too busy with the seasonal thongs to meet for lunch, I understand. But promise me you'll eat something?" She'd noticed her friend's usual appetite had disappeared since Nolan called her plump. Meg wasn't the least bit overweight, but she'd never been as naturally slim as her sisters. "If you've been starving yourself because that son of a—"

"Speaking of which. That 'son of a' is why I'm calling."

"Please tell me it's to say an anvil dropped out of the sky and hit him."

Meg laughed. "What is it with you and anvils?"

She shrugged, then realized Meg couldn't see. "Too much Wile E. Coyote in my formative years."

"Well, Nolan wasn't knocked unconscious by any falling cartoon props. But he did text me to say we can come get my stuff anytime after four today."

Meg had been outraged when she'd spoken to him on Monday and he'd told her he changed the locks. He'd refused to let her pick up her belongings without him being there to supervise.

"What does he think I'm going to do?" she'd demanded after ending the call. "Smash his TV set? Steal his spoons? Set his favorite jacket on fire? I've got more integrity than that!"

"Too bad," Dani had joked. "Because those all sounded like pretty decent ideas. Except, if we're going to steal something, the TV probably has a higher street value than the spoons."

"Anyway," Meg continued, "I already talked to Jamie." He was the brother she'd once tried to fix up with Dani; he was also the brother who owned an extended-bed pickup truck. "He can make this evening work. I know you wanted to come with me for moral support, but if you're busy…"

Dani did a mental rundown of the showings she'd planned to do, wondering if anything could be rearranged. Having seen how torn up Meg was this week, she didn't want her friend facing the man who'd broken her heart alone. Plus, Dani knew how protective Meg's siblings were. If Jamie found out the reason for the breakup was Nolan treating Meg like a brood mare, Dani might need to run interference to make sure no noses were broken.

"I can definitely help you out by five forty-five," Dani said. "But I think I might be able to manage earlier."

"You don't have to come with me," Meg stressed. "You've already done so much."

"Would you do the same for me?"

There was a brief silence.

Dani smiled. "That's what I thought." She was in the middle of disconnecting the call when Judy stuck her head into the office.

"Delivery for you, hon." She held a gorgeous tabletop bouquet. Instead of an elongated vase, the bunch of hydrangea, roses and orchids sat in a squared-off glass bowl, surrounded by smooth river rocks.

"Those are beautiful."

"No card that I can see," Judy said as she placed the floral arrangement on the corner of Dani's desk. "What is that at the bottom?"

Dani hadn't noticed, but sitting among the rocks was a small ceramic fairy holding a wand. The expression on her pixie face was mischievous, and she looked too young to be anyone's godmother, but the message was received. Sean had sent her flowers. Since several days had passed without hearing from him, she'd wondered if he'd finally put her behind him. She'd told herself that was what she wanted. But the brief flare of piercing joy she felt disproved that.

She sighed. "You know what? Let's leave these out in the general reception area so they can brighten everyone's day."

"You sure?"

"Yeah. I'm out of my office half the time anyway."

Judy tilted her head, regarding her. "This doesn't have anything to do with Hot Architect coming to see you last week, does it?"

"Bryce. The architect's name is Bryce." She had a newfound fixation for correctly identifying people. "But he's not the one who came into my office."

"Sure he was. I know what Hot—*Bryce* looks like. You could say I've made an informal study of him."

"He has a twin brother."

"There are *two* of them?" Judy's mouth dropped open. "Well, if that isn't proof of a benevolent higher power, I don't know what is. So do the flowers have anything to do with the twin?" she pressed. "I didn't know you were seeing anyone."

"I'm not," Dani said crisply. "And I think I hear the phone ringing."

It rang again, and Judy scowled. "Some days, getting my job done seriously cuts into my gossip schedule."

In general, Judy had a big heart. If anyone ever called

in sick with a cold or flu, they could expect a brief visit and a container of Judy's homemade chicken soup. But the woman did love her gossip. Since Judy couldn't keep a secret to save her life, there was no way Dani would tell her what was going on with Sean.

Especially since Dani wasn't even sure what was going on with him. Much as she'd tried not to, she'd been thinking of him a lot since that charged walk-through with the Andersens.

She picked up her phone. Sean had given her his business card, which was printed with his cell number. It seemed only right that she call and thank him for the flowers. But… She hesitated. If she expressed any gratitude, wasn't she just encouraging him?

Conversely, she could call to tell him he shouldn't have sent the flowers, but that was still her reaching out to him. She wasn't a fan of mixed messages. She made it through the rest of the day without phoning him, redirecting her focus to her clients and shifting her schedule so that she could drive Meg to Nolan's tonight. There was enough stuff that they'd need both Dani's car and Jamie's truck. She didn't allow herself any time to moon over a blue-eyed charmer with lax morals and great taste in flowers.

But as she crossed through the reception area on her way out for the night, she went to the vase that had been delivered. Shifting the box of flyers in her arm, she glanced around to see if anyone was looking. Then she plucked out the three-inch fairy, gently dropping it into her pocket and grinning the entire elevator ride down.

MEG KNOCKED, AND, standing next to her on the concrete stoop, Dani felt a twinge of sympathy. It had to be difficult, almost demeaning, to have to knock at the front door of a place you'd called home mere days ago. Even though they'd arrived at exactly the time Meg had texted, Nolan made them wait a few minutes before he opened the door.

He was a tall, slim guy with dark hair. Not bad-looking, despite a weak chin. When Dani had first met him, her only thought about his appearance was that his features made him look a little petulant. Now, she reconsidered her opinion, no longer blaming his features. Perhaps the problem was his attitude. Once he'd let them in, he stalked back to a desk in the corner and began typing on his laptop. He didn't even spare a cursory hi for Meg or ask how she was.

Meg sighed. "Come on. Bedroom's this way. We can box stuff up while we wait for Jamie."

He'd called to say he was stuck in traffic, but they could get started without him. They mostly needed Jamie to transport furniture and help carry heavy items. The two women had already made several trips to Dani's car before he finally rolled up in front of the house. Nolan watched the three of them lift an antique table Meg had inherited from her great-aunt without offering assistance, only a baleful glare.

It was odd—supposedly Nolan had loved Meg enough to pledge his entire life to her. Yet when she'd turned down his marriage proposal, his response was to sulk like a toddler. He hadn't tried to reconcile, wasn't doing a damn thing to win her back. His attitude was in stark contrast to Sean's. Sean Grayson hardly knew Dani, had only promised her a single night, yet he continued to court her, in his own stubborn, insufferable way.

Well, the flowers were actually beautiful. Maybe they didn't fall under the "insufferable" heading.

Dani was carrying a laundry basket full of books and DVDs out to the truck when the phone in her pocket dinged. "Hello?"

"Dani. Glad I caught you. It's Erik Frye." He sounded frazzled.

"Tough day?" she guessed.

"Tough day for my mom. She lives alone in Savannah, and she fell down her stairs today."

"I'm so sorry. Is she okay?"

"Bruised and battered, but X-rays show nothing's broken, thank God." He sighed heavily. "This is the third fall she's had since Christmas. We've been trying to talk her into selling that house, but she and Dad lived there for decades before he died. I think she feels like she'd be, I don't know, abandoning him if she leaves."

"Well, you and I know better than most, people get sentimentally attached to their homes." She'd seen sellers turn down lucrative offers because they didn't have the right feeling about certain buyers, couldn't envision the new people in "their" home.

"She's staying in the hospital tonight. I want to get down there, take care of her for the next couple of days and revisit the single-story ranch home discussion. My brother's in Ohio, so it's harder for him to go, and my sister's got her kids plus the benefit she's helping run this weekend. I hate to cancel on you for Saturday."

"Forget about me—your mom needs you. I completely understand."

"Would you be willing to go anyway? I paid for two tickets, and I'd love for them to be used. According to my sister, the fashion show will be entertaining. It's followed by dinner and dancing. The committee worked hard, and they're hoping for a strong turnout. Please take the tickets."

She looked back toward the house, thinking of how despondent Meg had been this week. It might be best for her friend's mental health if she got out and did something fun instead of being cooped up in Dani's depressing apartment all weekend.

"As it happens, Erik, I know someone who could use a few hours of fun."

WHEN SEAN'S CELL PHONE rang at noon on Saturday, he was standing in his galley-style kitchen making lunch. Turning down the burner underneath a pot of jarred pasta sauce, he dove for the cell on the far end of the counter. *Maybe this time...* Ever since he'd received confirmation of the florist's delivery, he'd been hoping to hear from Dani.

"Hello?"

"¿Qué pasa?" Alex greeted him. "Some of the guys are meeting to play basketball at the center. We'd planned a game of three-on-three, but we're one short. You free this afternoon?"

"Actually, no. I was eating a quick lunch, then headed out the door. I have a few errands to run and then I... promised some people I'd help with something today." That was all Alex needed to know. Sean didn't mind contributing his time to a worthy cause, but that didn't mean he was going to blithely hand his smart-assed friend a weapon of mass mockery.

"Okay. Guess I'll call Pete, then. You should feel special—you were our first choice."

"I feel very special. I'm writing about it in my diary even as we speak."

Alex snorted, then hung up.

In the silence that followed, Sean kicked himself for getting his hopes up that the caller would be Dani. He'd apologized, he'd flirted, he'd given her space, he'd sent her a gift. And what did he get in return? Radio silence. He blew out an exasperated breath. Where was the line between laudable persistence and being an ass who couldn't take a hint?

Hint taken, Danica.

If she had no interest in him, maybe he'd be wise to leave her alone—as Bryce had suggested last weekend. Taking any advice from his brother stuck in his craw. And knowing that he'd probably encounter his twin today, not to mention his ex-girlfriend, did nothing to boost his mood.

Sean spared a wistful thought for the basketball game he'd declined. Shooting hoops with the guys would be vastly preferable to the afternoon and evening ahead of him. The sacrifice was for a good cause, though. Maybe he couldn't scrawl his signature on a huge check the way some could, but he could donate his time.

After all, raising money to help feed kids beat the hell out of sitting around and waiting for his phone to ring.

"Ooh-la-la," Meg said as they sat waiting behind the other cars lined up at the valet stand. "I've never been to a country club before."

Dani had, but not this particular one. The club was so elite a person couldn't even view the website without logging in as a member first. She'd discovered that when she tried to confirm the driving directions.

"You think we're dressed okay?" Meg asked.

"You look beautiful." Her friend looked like a curvy, gothic take on a stained-glass window, but Dani was afraid that wouldn't come out sounding like the compliment it was. Meg's dress was see-through black lace with a handkerchief hem over a sheath of riotous colors. "Hey, if nothing else, I'll bet you have the very best underwear of any woman in the joint." Meg had come home late last night with a big bag of inventory she'd liberated from the store, declaring that, given their lousy luck lately, the two of them had earned some frivolous goodies.

"I, on the other hand, look like a very tall crayon," Dani joked. "Something in the 'brick-red' family." Most of the dresses she owned were too businesslike, so she'd gone with a monochromatic tunic and pants combo. With its high boat neck and three-quarter sleeves, her top was extremely conservative from the front. But the low drape in the back exposed a lot of skin. The billowy, wide-legged cut of the legs added some drama to the outfit, too.

Valets opened their car doors, and Dani stepped out into the sunshine. It was only four-thirty now, but the event would go into the evening.

"Danica, is that you?"

She turned to see Lydia Reynolds emerging from one of the cars behind them, accompanied by a bearded man who looked vaguely familiar. Dani realized that while she'd never met him, she'd seen his picture on promotional materials for his real-estate agency. They entered the country club as a group, with Dani making a concerted effort to discuss something other than real estate. She didn't want Meg to feel left out.

The charity event was taking place in two rooms—a formal dining room with a dance floor, and a smaller, adjacent room that was decorated with more festive flair. It had been set up to resemble a beach party, albeit a very expensive one on a private stretch of white sand, not the kind of informal bash where people roasted hot dogs over a bonfire. Unlike the tuxedoed wait staff who would serve dinner after the fashion show, the waiters circulating in here wore Hawaiian shirts and offered flutes of champagne as well as the event's signature "Hang Ten" cocktail. The room was dominated by a large runway with chairs on all sides.

Meg stared at the catwalk thoughtfully. "Think they'd ever be interested in doing a lingerie show? I could give someone my card. I'd only send the tasteful stuff," she added when Dani raised her eyebrows.

There were some club members at a table along a side wall, giving out more information about the organization they were supporting and trying to recruit volunteers for future events. Dani quickly discovered which one was Erik's sister and asked how their mother was doing; she also made a point of saying that the room looked great.

"Thank you so much," the other woman said. "I hate that Erik couldn't make it—I worry about him since the divorce, he needs more social interaction—but I'm glad his tickets aren't going to waste. You have fun this afternoon, and try a Hang Ten! They're yummy."

And strong. Dani hadn't heard all of the ingredients when a waiter gave another guest the recipe, but there were at least two types of rum, plus vodka. She suddenly flashed back to the silly game she and Sean had played, trying to pair up ideal cocktails with unlikely events.

"What are you grinning about?" Meg asked, sipping her drink. "You look like you're up to something."

"Oh, just remembering something goofy."

"Well, you need more goofy in your life," Meg declared. "You have a beautiful smile, and you don't use it enough. You're very work, work, work."

"Says the woman who put in sixty hours this week."

"True. But Marissa and I hosted a bachelorette party at the store and I wrote an article for our customer newsletter entitled 'If Your Boobs Could Talk.' I'm not worried *my* job will make me boring."

"Hey!" It was hard to sound indignant when she was giggling over Meg's article. Normally Dani wasn't a giggler. She blamed the Hang Ten. "I'm not boring."

They were still harassing each other when Lydia joined them, pointing out in hushed tones that one of the waiters was extremely hot. "He could be a male model," Lydia sighed. Dani had already surmised that Lydia's bearded "date" for the evening was just a colleague, not an actual date.

"Makes sense," Meg said. "Don't most aspiring models and actors have side gigs waiting tables until they get their big break?"

"I'd like to give him a break," Lydia said. "Or at least my phone number. I suppose that would be inappropriate since he's working."

"Have another Hang Ten," Meg suggested, tongue in cheek. "You'll stop caring about what's appropriate."

Lydia laughed. "If there weren't so many prospective clients and people I already do business with here, I might take that advice. As it is, I'm going to see where

I can track down a soda. The circulating waiters only have booze."

"Probably a ploy to make donors more generous," Dani said wryly. When the other woman went off in search of nonalcoholic libations, Dani told Meg, "There goes a woman with a healthy appreciation for the opposite sex. Every time I see her, she's lusting after a different guy."

Then again, last time they'd encountered each other, Lydia had been expressing lust for Sean. *Can't fault her taste.*

Dani sighed, aggravated to find herself thinking about him for the second time since she'd arrived. It was even worse at home. Why had she put that ceramic fairy on her nightstand, where it served as a constant reminder? Two weeks had passed since her night with Sean, and she still shivered at the memory of his touch.

Since she didn't seem to be getting over him, should she try getting past his lying to her? It was possible he truly regretted his error in judgment and had learned his lesson. Or was she trying too hard to rationalize her own weakness?

"You okay?" Meg asked.

"I miss him," Dani admitted.

Meg was such a good friend that, even though they hadn't been discussing Sean, she had no trouble following Dani's train of thought. "I know he made a mistake, but doesn't everyone? I moved in with Nolan, and that was a mistake. *You* agreed to marry Tate."

"In hindsight, those were regrettable decisions," Dani agreed. But that was the problem. She was afraid of making more decisions she'd have cause to regret. After only one night with Sean, he was taking up far too much of her concentration and emotional energy. Finding out he'd lied had hurt far more than it should have. If they dated and something else went wrong…

"Ohmigosh." Lydia suddenly reappeared, grabbing Dani's arm. "Did you know he was going to be here? Standing back by the palm tree with all the lights on it. Don't be obvious."

For a nonsensical moment, Dani thought she meant Sean but then realized Lydia didn't even know they'd been discussing him. She turned to glance casually over her shoulder. "Who am I looking for, exactly?"

"Your ex," Lydia said, her voice full of sympathy. "And the new missus."

IN THE CURTAINED area that served as backstage, Sean listened to the event emcee kick off the show with a few jokes. The elderly husband and wife team who'd founded Sunny Meals got ready to make their entrance. In keeping with the summer theme of their charity, the runway show was a playful look at warm-weather "fashions."

Sean wished desperately that *his* outfit could have been the husband's red, white and blue salute to the Fourth of July, complete with gaudy novelty sunglasses. Or, hell, even the wife's tennis dress would have been an improvement.

When the woman coordinating the ensembles had first handed him the swimsuit, he'd been appalled. "I told the woman on the phone I was fine with swim trunks. These don't qualify as trunks." The black shorts with their drawstring tie were extremely, well, *short*. "Was this Tara Blakely's idea?" Maybe participating in an event your ex helped organize was asking for trouble.

The wardrobe coordinator had beamed at him. "Actually, committee members made all decisions together. And this one was unanimous."

He stood backstage trying to psyche himself up by reminding himself that guys on the high school swim team had worn far skimpier suits. And what about Olympic swimmers? This was practically patriotic.

About the time he made peace with going out in front of a bunch of people in the suit, the coordinator returned to complete his humiliation. "I almost forgot these!" She handed him a pair of goggles, which he eagerly put on. Obscuring his face sounded pretty good right now. "Oh, no. You should wear them up on your head," she corrected. "And, for the finishing touch…"

That was when he noticed the bright yellow swim flippers.

"What, no speargun?" he asked sardonically. Charitable urges were all well and good, but why hadn't he just done another building project with Habitat for Humanity?

As he waited his turn, he thought about karma. He'd lied to a beautiful woman who didn't deserve it and now here he was, mostly naked, about to flap onto the runway in giant rubber fins.

Could be worse. After all, now that he and Tara had broken up, he rarely hung out with members of elite country clubs. So, the good news was, even if he looked like a moron, what did he care what the audience thought?

MEG WAS FUMING as only the best friend of a jilted woman could. "I can't believe he even has the nerve to show his face in the community," she whispered, glaring daggers toward the row where Tate and Ella sat. Luckily, the room's lights had been dimmed to maximize the spotlight on the runway. Dani didn't think her ex had even noticed she was here. "Men who ditch their fiancées for Scandinavian bimbos should be required to relocate."

Dani tried not to laugh out loud—onstage, the emcee was talking about the great cause that had brought them all here today. "We don't really have any evidence that she's a bimbo. And I'm not sure Finland is Scandinavian. Nordic, maybe?"

Music started and a silver-haired couple began making their way down the runway, hamming it up for the crowd. After them came a shapely woman in an Atlanta Braves replica jersey, hat and baseball pants. She carried a bat and had two black lines of glare-reducing grease beneath her eyes just like the pros. Following her was a ridiculously cute mother-daughter duo in matching bathing suits. When people saw the adorable toddler carrying a bucket and shovel, murmurs of "aw" sounded all around the room. They finished their turn on stage, and a man—or possibly a Greek god—appeared at the back of the catwalk. When he first appeared, his face was in shadows, but the spotlight hit every ridge of muscle on his sculpted abs.

Meg, who'd been leaning close to Dani to whisper commentary, suddenly sat bolt upright. "Oh, my." She jabbed Dani in the ribs. Hard. "Wait, is that the architect from your building?"

Dani swallowed, her mouth dry. "Worse. That's Sean." Every cell in her body recognized him.

On Dani's other side, Lydia Reynolds was too dumbstruck for words. She simply stared, mesmerized.

"I can't even be jealous," Meg whispered, "that you got to sleep with him. I'm just impressed you were brave enough. Must be intimidating as hell to get naked with someone who has a body like that."

She didn't recall intimidation during her night with him. Just eagerness, hunger, blinding arousal and bliss. It was easy to tell oneself, after the fact, that no mere mortal could be quite as perfect as she remembered Sean in fantasies. But, physically, he was sublime. Ogling him now, she was shocked she'd manage to resist him for two weeks. Future generations would speak in hushed tones of her willpower. *Or my stupidity.*

The closer he walked toward them, the more obvious the fins on his feet became, adding a comic touch to his normal predatory grace. *Flop flop flop.* Dani couldn't help it. A peal of laughter escaped.

For a moment, Sean froze on stage. Had he actually heard her over the other murmured conversations taking place in the dim room? No doubt half the females in here were exchanging admiring comments about the tall, dark and handsome man on the runway. This was a man who could easily have his pick of women. *But he wanted you.* It was a heady thought.

They hadn't spoken in days, and she hadn't acknowledged the flowers. Had his interest in her dimmed? If she walked up to him after the show, would he be happy to see her? She was so lost in imagined scenarios that she barely registered the rest of the show. Soon, the audience was clapping for the finale—the adult daughter of the country club's president decked out as a mermaid.

Guests were gently herded toward the dining room. Meg accepted another cocktail from a waiter standing in the doorway with a tray of drinks. Dani didn't need any alcohol. She was buzzed from the sight of a shirtless Sean. Assigned seats had been arranged with place cards, and it turned out that one of the women at their table had been in Meg's shop a few times. The two exchanged friendly small talk. Dani noticed that her friend's speech was occasionally slurred, but slightly enough that it could be passed off as Southern drawl.

Besides, plenty of other people had been enjoying the signature cocktails; Meg's periodic tripping over her tongue didn't stand out. She'd be fine as soon as she got some food in her stomach. In keeping with her postbreakup diet, however, she barely touched the first course. Waiters removed the salad plates and replaced them with entrées of herb-encrusted prime rib. Dani ate hers without tasting it, busily scanning the room to look for Sean. A number of the other amateur models were beginning to appear now that they'd changed into regular clothes. Where was he?

There. Her heart stuttered. Nope, that wasn't him. Even from across the dining room, she realized she was looking at Bryce. Aside from superficial differences like the kinds of clothes they wore or the way they styled their hair, the two men carried themselves differently. She was surprised they were both in attendance. Sean had given her the impression they didn't run in the same circles.

She went back to searching the room. Once she spotted him for real, looking devastatingly sexy in a black suit and white shirt unbuttoned at the collar, it occurred to her she would have found him more quickly if she'd simply looked for a throng of females instead of a lone man. He was surrounded by no fewer than four women, including Lydia Reynolds and a blonde with unnaturally full lips who stood very close and had a hand on his arm. Dani blinked. Was he here with a *date*?

Well, really, what had she thought—that he'd wait for her forever? *You told him you didn't want to see him again and that there was no chance you'd change your mind.* Apparently, of the two of them, Sean wasn't the only liar.

After watching the blonde in the bandage dress lead Sean to a table, Dani had made it a point to stop staring. Instead, she focused her attention on dessert, stabbing it rather savagely.

Face propped on her hand, Meg peered at her with concern. "Did that tiramisu do something to you personally?" she asked, stumbling a bit over the last word.

"Sorry." Dani pushed away the plate. "I think I've hit my quota on fun. Instead of staying for the dancing, how about we go home and get started on our movie marathon?"

"'Kay."

This was good. Go home, change into comfy clothes, try again to get Meg to eat. *And avoid watching Sean dance with a hot blonde date?* Okay, that was a perk, too.

As the DJ in the corner kicked off the after-dinner party with a Beach Boys tune, Dani made sure she and Meg both had their purses and cell phones. They bid their table companions goodbye and headed for the dining room exit, but they weren't quite fast enough to make a clean getaway.

"Danica?"

At the sound of Tate's voice, she squeezed her eyes shut. *Just kill me now.* She didn't want to make a scene by being rude to him, but she was feeling too drained to stand around making small talk. Maybe she could keep walking and pretend she hadn't heard him over the music and background party noise?

But Meg stopped dead in her tracks, whirling around. "Ooh! It's about time I gave him a piece of my mind for how he treated you."

As potentially entertaining as that would be to watch, especially given Meg's incongruous use of words like heck and darn, Dani shook her head. "Absolutely not. He isn't worth it."

Meanwhile, Tate was catching up to them. He flashed Dani a smarmy game-show host smile. "That *is* you. I'm so glad to see you out and about."

As opposed to what, sobbing quietly in her room while clutching a photo album of the two of them?

"And you look really good." He managed to make it more condescension than compliment. "You weren't leaving already, were you? It's still early."

"Not a chance," Meg said, pronouncing it *shance*. "We're…only goin' to powder our noses. Then we're gonna dance! With a whole bunch of men."

Tate spared her a withering glance before turning back to Dani. "Well, I suppose that's the benefit of bringing your little friend here as your date. You're available to—"

"Dani." A deep, familiar voice interrupted.

They all three turned, with varying degrees of surprise, to see Sean strolling up to them. He held a hand out toward her. "Care to dance?"

"If you don't, *I'm* taking him," Meg warned in an unsubtle whisper.

Stay here, on the receiving end of Tate's sham concern, or spend time in the arms of the sexiest guy in the room? No contest.

Dani curled her fingers through Sean's, a delighted zing shooting through her at the physical contact. "Lead the way."

11

Nodding politely to indicate that he was listening, Bryce Grayson surreptitiously checked his watch. He'd been dying to leave since before dinner, but his boss's wife was on the event committee. Seizing the first opportunity to bolt didn't seem like a good career move.

Then again, if he had bolted, he wouldn't be stuck listening to Dr. Hargrove, a local cardiologist, tell the same golf story Bryce had already heard twice this month. This was only marginally a step up from the dinner conversation, which had included a divorcée unsubtly hinting that Bryce should introduce her to Sean—*not likely*—and a namedropping couple who'd apparently met every Important Person who'd ever passed through the Atlanta area. By the time Bryce had finished dinner, he'd had a headache. The dance music wasn't helping.

Neither was the knowledge that Sean was in the ballroom. Bryce was unaccustomed to moving in the same social circles as his twin. Did others notice that he hadn't approached his own brother all night? Bryce had started to, but what was the point? His last two exchanges with Sean had become hostile pretty quickly.

While he hoped Sean would be more diplomatic in a public setting, he wasn't willing to take the risk.

When the doctor finally reached the conclusion of his story, Bryce offered what might have been his first genuine smile in hours. "So good to see you again, but I think I'm going to head home. Long week at the office," he added, trying to look fatigued rather than exuberant about his impending escape.

Bryce had only taken a few steps toward the door, however, when his brother's ex-girlfriend suddenly inserted herself in his path. "Tara." He nodded in greeting. "I understand you're on the committee for this event. Job well done."

"Thank you, but I'm afraid we're headed into fiasco territory. Ride to my rescue?"

Not if it involved anything like appearing publicly in an outfit as ridiculous as what Sean had worn. "What do you need?" he asked cautiously.

"Someone to run interference. The committee members worked their tails off to make this a perfect night, and I don't want it ruined by tacky people making a scene." She gestured toward the side of the dance floor. Two women and a man were involved in a heated conversation that appeared to be escalating. "I'd take care of it myself but I have to prevent another social disaster. Judge Waylan's wife *and* his girlfriend just headed toward the ladies' lounge."

Getting involved in the business of strangers wasn't exactly in Bryce's comfort zone. "You sure you don't want to delegate this to one of your committee members?" he hedged.

"And throw more estrogen on the fires of a potential chick fight? No." She looked up at him from beneath her lashes. "Besides, you've always had such an authoritative air about you."

Was he misreading the purr in her voice? The idea of his twin's ex hitting on him was distasteful enough to propel him toward the altercation brewing by the dance floor. "All right, I'm on it." He'd see what he could do to stem brewing trouble, and then he was definitely leaving.

Ahead of him, a woman with curly red-gold hair was angrily addressing a short man, poking him in the chest with her finger. A second woman clutched his arm, making rebuttals in a heavy accent.

Bryce cleared his throat. "Is there a problem here, folks?"

The man in the tableau looked embarrassed to have a witness. "No problem, just, um, catching up with—" he eyed the curly-haired spitfire in the lacy black dress "—an old friend."

"Friend?" The woman on his arm sneered. "She is a drunken lunatic!"

The alleged lunatic balled her hands into fists at her sides. "Why you—"

"Excuse me, miss." Bryce interjected himself between the two females. Other than create a physical barrier, he wasn't sure what to do. The sudden change from one song to another inspired him. "Would you like to dance?"

Waving away the couple with a hand behind his back, he focused on distracting the woman with the wide brown eyes and red-gold hair. Now that he got a better look at her, he noticed that she had a creamy, porcelain complexion and the face of an angel. Ironic, given what he'd witnessed of her temperament.

She met his gaze, seeming bewildered. "Whoa. I'm seeing double."

"Have you had a lot to drink?" Maybe he needed to get her to a chair.

She paused as if taking a mental tally, then shrugged. "Irrelevant."

"Not if you're having double vision," he said gently.

"I see two of you because there are two of you." She gripped his shoulders and turned him toward the dance floor, pointing.

Following the direction she indicated, he spotted Sean in the crowd. "Oh. Right. We're twins."

She gave him a look of exaggerated patience. "Duh. You're the Bryce one, right?"

This was the strangest conversation he'd had all night, but at least it wasn't boring. "Yeah. I'm the Bryce one. And who might you be?"

"Meg."

"Could I interest you in a cup of coffee?" he offered. "Maybe some dessert to go with it?" He figured adding chocolate as an enticement sounded kinder than admitting he was trying to sober her up.

"Dessert." She sighed wistfully. Suddenly, she reached for him, moving much faster than he'd expected for a woman who was swaying slightly, and pressed his hand to her lace-covered hip. "What do you think? Too plump?"

"I… What?"

"I need a man's opinion." For a moment, the expression in her doe eyes got less vague. "You are a man."

He didn't know if it was the undercurrent of appreciation in her voice or the soft, full curve of her beneath his fingers that sent a rush of heat through him. He did, however, know that it was inappropriate to be groping a stranger.

"Do my hips inherently fill men's heads with thoughts of babies?" she demanded.

Thoughts of how babies were made, perhaps.

"Um…no?" He tugged his hand away, trying to regain his composure. He'd done his job of averting a scene. He was free to go now. But he was troubled by the trace of sadness in her gaze. He realized he wanted, quite badly, to see her smile. "Nice dress." It was unlike anyone else's.

"You should see my underwear," she said absently. The bizarre statement was matter-of-fact, no whisper of come-on in her voice.

He had no idea how he was supposed to respond, which was just as well, since he couldn't find his voice anyway.

Standing on her tiptoes, she peered around him, tottering on her high heels. Bryce's hands came up automatically to steady her. Maybe he should stay close to her. In case she needed help.

"What are you looking for?" he asked.

"Tate got away before I got a chance to tell him he's an excrement head."

His lips twitched. "Interesting way of putting it."

"I don't swear. It's a rule." She lifted her chin. Her imperious expression was surprisingly effective, given that she didn't even reach his shoulder and she was wobbling. "People need to respect the rules."

He nodded. "I myself am a firm believer in them."

That earned him the smile he'd wanted. Her lips curved in an approving grin, making her eyes twinkle. The way she looked at him, he suddenly felt a foot taller.

"Rule follower, huh? I…" She blinked as if she'd forgotten what she was going to say. Then she yawned, and it occurred to him that someone should probably take her home.

"Did you come here with someone tonight?" he asked. Even as he voiced the question, he sincerely hoped the answer was no. In fact, he so badly wanted her to be here without a date that it startled him. Since when was he attracted to unpredictable strawberry blondes who made muttered comments about under-wear?

"Came with my friend," she said sleepily. Once again, she gestured toward the dance floor. "Danica."

Crap. "Danica Yates?" He frowned, wondering how much it would count against him that Ms. Yates disliked him. Although, upon second glance, he realized Danica was the woman dancing with Sean. Had the real-estate agent reversed her ruling on Grayson men?

"Danica is my best friend," Meg said, her angelic face crinkling into a fierce scowl. She pressed a palm to her forehead. "And you're just… I shouldn't even be talking to you."

"Wait, I—"

"No, I think I need to get home," she said in a mo-ment of clarity. She headed toward the dance floor, pre-sumably to let her ride know it was time to leave. Then she paused, giving him one last sleepy smile over her shoulder. "Goodbye, Hot Architect."

She knew he was an architect? He was surprised Danica had bothered mentioning it. Then the rest of what she'd said clicked, prompting a grin. *She thinks I'm hot?*

UNSURE WHAT TO say to Sean—and biting back the ques-tion *Is that skinny blonde I saw you with your date?*—

Dani had followed him silently to the dance floor. The loud music provided a convenient excuse not to talk. For the first few measures of the song, she simply gave into the impulse to melt against him and enjoy the moment.

But he had questions of his own. "You were really going to marry that guy? He seems like a putz."

Too true. She sighed. "He wasn't always so self-important. I think getting promoted and Ella falling for him went to his head." It was probably for the best Sean had interrupted when he had, before Dani was provoked into cutting Tate and his ego down to size. A petty part of her had enjoyed Tate's expression—and how he'd had to crane his neck to look up at Sean—when his "poor Dani" act had been interrupted. "I'm glad you ran into me when you did."

"It wasn't coincidental. I asked Lydia Reynolds if she knew where you'd gone, and she said you'd been cornered by your cretin ex."

"You knew I was here?" she asked softly. The few times she'd glanced his direction, he'd been busy with admirers.

He nodded. "I heard you laugh during the fashion show. You're a saint, by the way, not to have mentioned those damn fins yet."

"Now I'm worried I have an obnoxiously distinct laugh," she joked. "How else could you have recognized it over the music and noise of the crowd?"

His gaze held hers. "I think I could pick you out of a hundred voices or a thousand faces. Dani, I…"

Her breath caught in her lungs, and she swayed even closer to him. Hunger lit his gaze, and an answering hunger surged to life inside her. He stared at her mouth, and a tingly sensation spread from her lips, in anticipation of his kiss, to other parts of her body, lower and stronger until she found herself shifting restlessly, trying in vain to alleviate the ache.

With a muffled groan, he cupped the back of her head. "If you can't forgive what I did, tell me right now. I'll walk away, and that will be the end of it. Otherwise—"

"I can," she blurted, her voice unrecognizably breathy as she tightened her grip on him. "I forgive you."

He brushed his tongue over the seam of her lips, then into her mouth with a boldness that reminded her of the way he made love—confident and skilled, so adept at knowing what she liked that she wanted it to go on forever. Maybe it would have, if they hadn't backed into the couple next to them. *We can't do this here.* They should go to her apartment and—

Oh, Lord, she'd completely forgotten about her temporary roommate.

Breaking off the kiss, she glanced around. "I am a terrible friend. I have to find Meg. She had several of those Hang Tens on an empty stomach. I mean, she's fine as long as she's not driving, but I should probably discourage her from drinking any more of them."

"That's being a caring, concerned friend." He tapped her nose lightly. "You're not terrible at all." From his elevated vantage point, he scanned the room. "There she is."

He caught her hand in his, the simple act filling her with joy. On their first date, they'd pretty much gone from verbal foreplay to energetic sex. They'd skipped the smaller, yet surprisingly poignant, milestones.

Meg was weaving her way toward them. "Dani? Not to interrupt, but I think I'm go to ready."

Dani draped an arm around her friend's shoulders. "Or, loosely translated, ready to go?"

"That, too."

"Why don't I walk you ladies out to your car?" Sean volunteered.

Meg stuck her hand out in the apparently sudden realization that they'd never officially met. "I'm Meg Rafferty, Dani's best friend in the world. And if you ever make her cry again? I have more than enough siblings to provide me an alibi *and* help hide the body."

He flinched. His gaze darting back to Dani. "You cried over me?"

"Um…no comment." Dani had grown up never quite comfortable sharing her more sensitive moments with the Major. As an adult, she preferred to keep that side of herself hidden.

Dani and Sean each gave their vehicle tickets to the man at the valet stand. They stood on either side of Meg while they waited, in case she needed the physical support.

Over the top of Meg's head, Sean gave her a look of such fierce anticipation that it warmed her to her toes. "How soon can I see you again? A guy on my crew is having a birthday party tomorrow, but I'm free Monday night."

She bit the inside of her lip. "I have some evening showings for a client who has trouble getting away during the day. Tuesday?"

His face fell. "I'm supposed to— You can come with me," he interrupted himself. "My parents came back from Hawaii with a ton of pictures, but the last time I went over to look at them, Dad fell asleep midway through. According to Mom, we still have one hundred and forty seven to go. In the interest of full disclosure, Bryce might be there, too."

The idea didn't bother her as much as it would have a week ago. After all, noticing Bryce had led her indirectly to Sean. Despite the convoluted path, she was inclined to feel grateful. "Your parents won't mind a total stranger horning in on a family night?"

"Are you kidding? My mom will be *thrilled*."

She returned his smile, suddenly very eager for Tuesday and way too many tropical photos. "Then it's a date."

"Do I look okay?" Dani wanted to look nice, but not overdressed. She'd pulled her hair into a curly ponytail and paired a deep green short-sleeved top with black jeans.

Sitting at the foot of Dani's bed, Meg laughed. "I can't believe how nervous you are about this. The guy's completely smitten with you. You could show up in a burlap sack and flip-flops, and I'm not sure he'd even notice."

"I don't know about that. Besides, it isn't just Sean. It's his parents." When he'd asked her to go with him to their house, she'd been so eager to see him again that she'd automatically agreed. But now she was second-guessing herself. Who agreed to meet the parents on the second date?

Then again, not everyone got naked on the first date. Lord knew, she usually didn't. "Everything about this relationship seems out of order. Chronologically, speaking."

Meg shrugged. "You did everything in normal, logical order with Tate. Maybe it's good you're shaking things up."

A knock sounded at the door while Dani was fishing through her jewelry box for earrings.

"I'll get the door." Meg stood. "It's a perfect opportunity to give my 'hurt her and I'll end you' warning."

"You already did that," Dani reminded her. "On Saturday."

"Oh." Meg's forehead crinkled as she tried to remember. "Well, now he can hear the sober version."

Dani chuckled. Meg had been making more jokes over the past couple of days and seemed to be regaining her appetite. She was definitely doing better her second week post-Nolan than she had her first.

In the next room, Meg and Sean exchanged pleasantries. Just the sound of his low voice made Dani quiver inside. Even during the weeks when she'd told herself she shouldn't be thinking about him, she'd never been successful at banishing him from her mind. Now that she'd given herself permission to pursue something with him, he was always there, at the forefront of her thoughts.

She frequently found herself smiling for no reason. Although no one at work had said anything directly, she knew they'd noticed a change in her demeanor. And at softball practice, when the volunteers split the girls into two groups to work on different skills, one twelve-year-old had declared, "I want to go to the station with the happy coach."

That's me. The happy coach.

A broad smile on her face, she went into the living room, loving that everything she felt was mirrored in Sean's expression when he saw her.

"Have her home by eleven," Meg teased. "It's a school night." She then disappeared into the kitchen, giving the two of them a chance to greet each other with more than smiles.

Sean crossed the living room in two long strides, and her pulse quickened. He crushed her to him, his hands sliding beneath the hem of her shirt and along her lower back as he kissed her. Shivery pleasure danced up her spine, and she gave in to the impish urge to grab his butt.

He pulled back with a raised eyebrow. "Keep that up, and we will be *very* late to my parents' house."

She grinned. "Complaining?"

"Begging."

She was still laughing when they left her apartment. They talked about work during the drive. She told him about a subdivision she'd been to today, and he sniffed in feigned derision.

"Sounds like an okay place if your clients want substandard. We both know Magnolia Grove is superior."

"It definitely has a sexier builder. But I'm not sure my clients are going to factor that into their decision. By the way, if Lydia Reynolds shows up again, you might want to discreetly let her know you're taken. That woman has designs on you."

Sean gave her a purely male smile, self-satisfied and irresistible. "Taken, huh?"

"I don't share." While it was impossible to know where seeing each other would lead, as long as they were dating, he was hers. "Probably an only child thing."

"Not necessarily. I grew up with a brother, and I have that selfish streak, too. Want you all to myself." The look he flashed her from the driver's seat was so hotly possessive her breath caught.

"Stop it," she muttered. At this rate, she'd be too turned-on to manage conversation with his parents.

"What am I supposed to stop doing, exactly?"

"Looking…" So sexy that she wanted to lick him up with a spoon? "At me," she finished weakly.

"Not a chance. It's my new favorite pastime."

"Okay." Since she felt the same about him, she couldn't really complain. "But do you have to keep looking at me like you're picturing me naked?"

His smile was wolfish. "You're not always naked. Sometimes there are shoes. And corsets."

She filed that information away for the next time she was in Meg's shop.

Whenever Dani arrived at a house she'd never visited before, it was habit to evaluate the curb appeal. The Graysons' modest ranch home sat on a well-maintained lot. The grass was verdant and freshly cut, and although the time-worn porch could use some TLC, potted flowers and a set of padded wicker chairs added an attractive splash of color.

"My brother's car isn't here," Sean said as they rolled into the driveway. "Maybe we'll be lucky, and he won't show."

"The two of you really don't get along, huh?"

He removed the key from the ignition. "A month ago, I would have told you that we get along in a strained sort of way. We weren't fighting, but we hardly spoke. The day I met you, I was leaving a birthday present in his office. Looking back, it feels like it was my last ditch effort to close the gap between us. I don't even know if he liked it. Things are getting worse lately. We argue more."

She considered this. "Are you sure that constitutes 'worse'?" At his puzzled look, she added, "Arguing involves talking. It's a kind of communication." Very loud communication, if the periodic disagreements between Rafferty siblings were anything to go by.

"That's an optimistic way of looking at it."

Grinning, she opened her car door. "I've been in a much more optimistic mood the past few days."

As they walked up the sidewalk, fingers interlaced, Sean said, "Usually, Mom doesn't even wait for me to get to the front door. She just meets me on the porch. This is her showing restraint because I've brought a guest. She's probably going out of her mind with curiosity on the other side of the door."

Sure enough, his knuckles had barely touched the wood when the door swung open. A woman with silver-streaked hair and youthful eyes beamed up at them.

"Hey, Mom." Sean bent down to kiss her cheek. "Dad knocked down any walls lately?"

Before she could answer, Mr. Grayson joined them in the foyer. He was as tall as Dani's father, which was saying something, had graying blond hair and hound-dog eyes, the kind Dani thought gave people an indefinably sad expression even when they were perfectly happy. Physically at least, husband and wife were polar opposites.

"Danica, these are my parents, Steve and Keely Grayson. Mom, Dad, this is my...Dani."

"It's so wonderful to meet you." Keely shook her hand enthusiastically. To her son, she said in a stage whisper, "The flowers worked?"

Dani grinned. "The flowers were lovely."

Behind them, there was a quick rap at the door, then Bryce stepped inside. "Hey, sorry I'm—" He drew up short at the sight of Dani, obviously not expecting to see her.

Keely waved everyone into the kitchen. "Dinner's almost ready. To get us in the mood for the Hawaiian pictures, I made pineapple-glazed pork. Dani, you aren't vegetarian or anything, are you?"

Thinking about the steak salad she'd polished off for lunch, she almost laughed. "No, ma'am."

They all pitched in to help carry dishes to the table and fill glasses. It was a different dynamic than the boisterous family dinners Dani had experienced with the Raffertys, and not just because Meg had a bigger family than Sean. There were no introverts in the Rafferty household. Everyone was talking and laughing and, occasionally, arguing at once. Here, it quickly became clear that Sean and his mother were used to carrying conversation. Mr. Grayson listened, his affection for both of them obvious, but didn't contribute much. Bryce was quiet, too.

"So, Dani," Keely began, "how did you and Sean meet?"

Dani swallowed her bite of homemade roll with a gulp. "I, uh…I work in the same building as Bryce." Across the table, the architect was studying her with an unreadable expression. Surely he wouldn't mention that Dani hadn't been able to tell the twins apart?

Sean squeezed her shoulder. "I had the good luck to run into her when I was dropping off a birthday present."

"Which I've been meaning to thank you for," Bryce said gruffly. "It…means a lot to me."

Next to her, Sean went rigid with surprise. "You're welcome."

There was a pause, as if even Keely didn't know what to say. Or maybe she was so glad to see her sons share a courteous moment that she wanted to savor it.

But then she asked if Dani had ever been to Hawaii, and conversation turned to vacation stories, including the ill-advised Grand Canyon road trip when Major Yates had thought ten days in a car with his preteen daughter was a good bonding opportunity.

When they were done with the meal, Sean volunteered himself and Dani to clean up the kitchen while his mom readied the picture presentation. "It's the least we can do, since you cooked." Beneath the table, his hand dropped to Dani's thigh and she knew he was trying to get a few minutes alone with her.

"Oh, I can't ask Dani to do dishes," Keely protested. "She's a guest."

"I really don't mind," Dani said.

Keely beamed. "And here I was afraid he'd never meet a nice girl. Sean, you feel free to bring her back anytime."

Their bid for a few minutes alone went awry when Bryce didn't follow his parents to the living room. Instead, he remained in the kitchen with them, awkwardly silent.

Sean and Dani exchanged glances. "Doesn't Mom need your help hooking her computer to the TV?" Sean prompted.

Bryce shook his head, looking distracted. "I only had to show her how the first time. She's got it now."

Dani had heard Sean talk about his brother being "the smart one," but it occurred to her that Bryce was pretty damn clueless in some matters.

"I really did like the print," Bryce said, handing his brother an empty casserole dish.

"So you mentioned." There was a note of suspicion in

Sean's tone, as if he questioned why his aloof twin was suddenly being nice. "Something on your mind, bro?"

"Some*one*. I've...I can't stop thinking about a woman I met."

Sean broke into a wide grin. "Really? It's hell, isn't it? No offense," he told Dani.

"None taken." She arched an eyebrow. "You think *I* was overjoyed when my brain turned into the all-Sean, all-the-time channel?"

"I still can't believe you forgave him," Bryce mused. "After the way he—"

"She was there," Sean interrupted. "She doesn't need the recap."

"Sorry." Bryce leaned against a kitchen counter. "My point is, there were obstacles and you overcame them. I've never done anything unkind toward this woman, but she said she shouldn't even talk to me. That's not a good sign, right?"

"So you need my help." Sean looked equal parts flabbergasted and smug over this turn of events. "Advice on how to win her over?"

"No. Actually, I was hoping for Danica's help. It's your friend," he told her. "Meg. We chatted at the charity dinner."

Her eyes widened. "You did?" Frankly, she couldn't imagine Bryce, the architect of few words, casually chatting with anyone—much less her extroverted friend who'd erred on the side of inebriation that night.

"She's beautiful. And funny." He didn't smile, but the corners of his eyes crinkled. "And very loyal to you. It's obvious the two of you are close. Would you be willing to give me her number? Or, at the very least, her last name?"

Was that such a good idea? Meg had been through a rough time already. And she'd dated more than one guy who'd decided her effusive personality was too much for him. Bryce was naturally reserved and skewed toward the judgmental.

"I don't know." The disappointment in his expression gave her a moment's guilt, but her allegiance was to Meg, not him. Inspiration struck in the form of a compromise. "I'll tell you where she works, though. Vivien's Armoire. You can find her there just about every day of the week."

If he was man enough to track her down amid the push-up bras and crotchless tap pants, then maybe he deserved a shot.

"I'm glad you came with me tonight," Sean said as he turned into the parking lot of Dani's apartment complex. "My parents really liked you."

No kidding, she thought numbly. At first, she'd appreciated how welcome Mrs. Grayson made her feel. But by the end of the evening, Keely had been dropping unsubtle hints that, when Dani got married, Hawaii would make a lovely honeymoon destination. Even hearing the word *honeymoon*, so soon after the one she hadn't taken, was discomfiting.

She'd debated telling Sean's mom they weren't that serious—tonight was only their second date!—but it didn't seem like a reminder that should come from her. So she'd waited to see if Sean would good-naturedly ask his mom to knock it off. He, on the other hand, hadn't seemed bothered. Perhaps he was just more laid-back on the topic of weddings, not being the one who'd recently returned a bunch of bridal-shower and engagement gifts, but she'd suddenly wondered if they were both on the same page.

"Your parents are nice." She stared out her window, searching for a way to voice her feelings that didn't make her sound as if she were overreacting. "And I had a good time. On the subject of us, though... You're okay with taking this slow, right?"

He parked near the corner of the building, a few yards from her front door. "Of course. I'm grateful you're no longer angry with me, but I know earning trust is a process. I don't want to rush you." He got out of the car and came around to open her door. "Besides, your apartment's pretty much at maximum capacity. I wasn't expecting you to invite me to stay the night with Meg here recuperating."

Wait, did he think her request to take things slow meant she wasn't ready to have sex again? Because actually—

"Did you have any idea she and my brother had talked?" he asked. "Have to say, Bryce caught me off guard with that."

"Me, too."

"If he asks her out, I hope she doesn't say yes right away." Sean snickered. "He was so pompous about my being hung up on you. Couldn't understand why I just didn't walk away."

Despite her reservations about making any long-term romantic plans, she was touched by his reluctance to give up on her. She grazed her knuckles over his cheek. "I'm glad you don't give up easily."

He turned his head, pressing a quick kiss against her hand. "Not when the reward for perseverance is you."

12

"So?" Meg stood in the doorway to Dani's room, where she'd apparently been waiting while Dani changed into pajamas and brushed her teeth. "How did it go? Were you able to avoid mention of how you seduced their son the day you met him? After you'd been gone a couple of hours, I figured it was safe to assume they hadn't labeled you a harlot and booted you out of their house."

"More like they were on the verge of asking me to call them Mom and Dad." Dani sat cross-legged on her bed. "Well, Mrs. Grayson was anyway. She did most of the talking on their behalf."

"That's so great that she liked you. One thing I will not miss about Nolan is his mother. She always acted like the age difference between us meant I was too immature for her worldly son." She gave a lopsided smile. "Maybe next time, I'll go for someone younger. Could be fun to have a boy-toy."

Dani didn't get the sense that "fun" was how most people described Bryce Grayson, but she couldn't forget the way his eyes lit up when he'd mentioned her friend.

"Your name came up tonight, by the way. Seems you made quite an impression on Bryce."

"Oh?" Meg kept her voice neutral, but telltale color stained her cheeks. "A good impression, or a 'who let *her* into the club?' impression?"

"Definitely good. Can I infer from the blush that he made an equally favorable impression? How come you didn't mention that you'd talked to him?"

Meg cast her gaze downward, suddenly fascinated by the nondescript beige carpeting. "Noticing that he's attractive felt like betraying you. You wanted him first."

"First of all, you'd have to be blind *not* to notice he's attractive. And I hardly knew the guy." As evidenced by her confusing him with someone else. "Whatever thoughts I may have had about him at one time, you know I'm not interested in Bryce anymore."

"Yeah, but you're dating his twin brother. Wouldn't it be awkward if I pursued a guy who's identical to your boyfriend?"

"This may sound weird, but the more time I spend with Sean, the less he looks like Bryce. They're really different."

Meg took a second to process that, then shook her head. "It's a moot point anyway. I ran into him the one time, but it isn't as though I frequent country clubs."

"I mentioned where you work," Dani admitted. "I don't know if he'll look you up or not, but he's invested enough to ask about you."

Meg giggled. "You remember when I went through that phase of trying to set you up with Jamie because I wanted us to be sisters-in-law? I suppose if we eventually married brothers, I could still get my wish."

Dani flopped back on the bed with a groan. "What

is it with all you people who have marriage on your minds?"

"It was just hypothetical."

"Still. I couldn't be less interested in thinking about that kind of commitment right now." If ever. "I thought I knew Tate. We were together for years, and I narrowly escaped hitching myself to a cheat and a liar. You don't celebrate an escape by looking for new traps. All I want is a little fun."

"Well, that's how love gets you," Meg said philosophically. "You start out having fun with someone, enjoying each other so much that one day, out of the clear blue sky—"

"Love hits you like an emotional anvil?" Dani rolled her eyes. "Jeez, sign me up for that."

"TEARJERKER OR ACTION MOVIE?" Sean asked when Dani opened her door Friday night. The latest in a superhero franchise was vying for lead at the box office with a deeply emotional film already getting Oscar buzz.

Dani snorted. "Like I want to pay thirteen dollars so I can sit in a crowded theater and cry off my eye makeup? Action, please."

He kissed her hello. "My kind of girl."

She grabbed a lightweight sweater in case the air-conditioned theater got too chilly and followed him outside. As she was locking the front door, the phone in her purse sounded. She checked to see if the call was from Meg. Usually her friend was home from work by now.

But it was her dad's number that flashed across the screen, which surprised her. Other than a flurry of concerned calls surrounding the wedding date, the Major wasn't really a phone person.

"Hey, Dad."

There was a pause on the other end of the line. "Danica. Are you…are you busy?"

Her gaze flicked to Sean. "I do have plans tonight. Did you need something?" He sounded strange, lacking his usual crisp, commanding intonation.

"No," he said too quickly. "Just wanted to hear your voice."

The more he spoke, the easier it was to detect the slur in his words. Belatedly, she recalled the date and its significance to her father. He hadn't let himself grieve in front of her often, but some years had been worse than others. "Daddy, have you been drinking?"

"I'm over twenty-one, Danica Leigh."

She moved the phone away from her face a moment. "Can we make a stop on the way to the theater? Well, not on the way in the strictest sense." They would miss the coming attraction previews for sure. "Dad, you sit tight. I'll be there soon."

Ending the call, she slid into the passenger seat of Sean's SUV with a worried sigh. "It's the anniversary of my mom's death," she said quietly. She rarely remembered, except when her father had one of his spells. "I think Dad's been drinking." First Meg at the country club and now this. "I swear not all the people in my life are lushes. You're catching us on a bad week."

Sean's hand dropped to her thigh. "People make questionable decisions when they're hurting. Hell, I'm living proof that people make questionable decisions, period."

She gave him directions to her dad's place, keeping one eye on the time. They were going to miss more than the previews. Maybe they could go to the later showing.

It took them about half an hour to reach the duplex where her father lived. The entire neighborhood was populated with retirees, and the parking lot was full of Buicks and Cadillacs from a bygone era. Not bothering to knock, she let herself in with her spare key.

"Dad? It's me. I'm here with a friend."

There was a shattering crash and some swearing from the next room. "In the kitchen," her father called back. The pungent scent of whiskey wafted down the hall to greet them. He must have knocked over a bottle. At least that meant there was less left for him to actually drink.

"He never does this," she told Sean, aware that the circumstances under which they were meeting each other's parents were radically different. Her family might only be made up of two people, but between her and her father, they had plenty of baggage.

When they walked into the kitchen, they found the Major trying to clean up spilled whiskey and broken glass. Photo albums were spread across the wooden, two-seater table.

"Daddy?"

The Major whirled, years of training and honed reflexes momentarily overcoming the booze. "Dammit. You shouldn't have to see me like... You look so much like her." He squinted, trying to peer past her shoulder into the dark hall behind her. "That better not be Tate with you. Lowlife cheating—"

"This is Sean Grayson. He's a friend. He's going to get you some water while I clean this up. You sit down," she said firmly. Of the three of them, her father was the only one barefoot.

She put her hands on his shoulders and gently steered

him toward a chair. He seemed too preoccupied with Sean's presence to notice.

"Are *you* a lowlife cheat?" the Major asked.

"No, sir."

"Good. Dani deserves better."

"I couldn't agree more, sir." Sean leaned over, studying one of the open albums while Dani got the broom and dustpan out of the pantry. "This must be your wife? She's very beautiful." Glancing in Dani's direction, he added, "You do look just like her."

A fact she well knew. It had been evident since she hit puberty that she was going to grow into the spitting image of a mother she'd barely known and couldn't remember. It was disorienting at times, to look at photos and see a face that mirrored her own. Then again, what must Sean's life be like, to stare into Bryce's face and see contempt or annoyance reflected on his own features?

Major Yates dropped his hand to one plastic-protected page. "She was my soul mate." His expression turned dreamy for a moment, his smile making him look years younger. "It's such a blessing to find that one person you were meant to be with."

Dani bit her lip, her eyes welling with tears at her dad's loneliness. Was he right? From a purely selfish standpoint, since it meant being born, she was glad he'd married her mother. But if he hadn't been so convinced that Gina Yates had been his "one and only," would he be remarried now? Growing old with someone who cared for him instead of drinking alone with only faded pictures for company?

He'd told Dani all during her adolescence that one day she'd find her special someone. As she'd entered her midtwenties, she'd begun to question that belief. When Tate had proposed, she'd thought she'd finally met her fabled match. She didn't want her breakup with Tate to leave her cynical—he wasn't entitled to hold that much sway over her. Yet, as she stepped gingerly across shards of broken glass and watched her father's equally broken expression, she wondered if perhaps *not* finding that one special person could be a blessing, too.

"I'M SORRY ABOUT the movie," Dani said as Sean made the turn into her apartment complex. "I know pizza and poker with my father wasn't the plan."

He shot her a grin. "I haven't had so many dates chaperoned by parents since I was fourteen." When she didn't laugh, he added, "I didn't mind. Really. This gives me an excuse to ask for a rain check on the movie and see you again soon."

Dani couldn't find Meg's car in the lot. When they walked inside the apartment, it was all dark except for the entryway nightlight.

She smacked a palm to her forehead, her memory belatedly kicking in. "Meg's hosting a bridal shower at the shop tonight! She told me days ago that she'd be out late, but I forgot." Possibly because she had a mental block when it came to anything bridal.

"They have those at lingerie shops?" he asked, sounding intrigued. "I thought showers were more Sunday dresses and mini-sandwiches while the bride-to-be opens plates and monogrammed towels."

"What a sadly narrow mind," she chided. "My bridal shower—" That was so not what she wanted to think about right now. "Suffice it to say, Meg's my best friend, so it was a bit more creative and less G-rated than what you describe. Now." She clutched the front of his shirt in both hands. "Do you want to stand around discussing potential shower gifts, or do you want to make the most of our time alone in a roommate-free apartment?"

He backed her to the nearest wall, leaning in with agonizing slowness, each heartbeat an eternity before their lips touched. But his teasing finesse didn't last long. When her tongue slid against his, he pressed into her, deepening their kiss, his mouth moving on hers with ravenous need.

He dropped his hands to her ass and lifted her. With her legs wrapped around his waist, he carried her toward the bedroom. The motion of his long strides, the jostling friction between her thighs, sent her soaring into a state of heightened sensitivity. By the time her feet touched the floor again in her room, she was nearly too aroused to stand.

Taking a moment to catch his breath, he flashed her a lopsided grin. "I have some very fond memories of this room."

So did she. Yet she also vividly recalled the last time they'd been here together, when he'd admitted who he was and she'd felt like twelve degrees of idiot. She shrank from the recollection, wanting to savor being with him now.

"Hey." There was genuine delight in his voice. "You kept her."

She followed his gaze to the tiny winged fairy on the nightstand, the one that had been nestled in the floral arrangement.

"I was afraid you might throw her out," he admitted. "Or refuse delivery of the flowers altogether." The note of vulnerability in his voice tugged at her heart, making it easier to banish unpleasant memories and her lingering fear of being made a fool. She wasn't the only one emotionally exposed here.

He brushed his fingers over the slope of her neck. "I wish I'd sent you flowers today. Then I could run the petals over your skin."

"Nice thought, but I want to feel your touch without anything between us." Not even the fine velvet of rose petals.

"Then we should really do something," he murmured against her lips, "about all these clothes."

There was no more talking then, only fervent kisses as they undressed one another, exploring each other's bodies and doing their best to make up for the weeks they'd missed each other.

Sean sat on the edge of her bed, shucking his socks and then his briefs. She stared unabashedly, loving every line of his amazingly sculpted body. Her gaze swept over the dark hair on his chest down to his jutting erection. She considered sinking to her knees and tasting him, but he reached for her before she got the chance, toppling her onto the mattress with him.

With a muffled squeal, she landed astride him and decided this was good, too. More than good. Sprawled across him, she kissed him hungrily while his hands stroked and kneaded. Fire spread through her, arousal a pulse at her core, her nipples puckered into tight buds. She propped herself up to give him better access to her breasts, and he happily took advantage.

He cupped her breasts together, his thumbs teasing both peaks, until she was nearly mindless. She bucked against him, so slick that all it would have taken was a slight movement of his hips to be inside her. Temporarily regaining sense, she pulled a condom out of the nightstand. When he reached for the packet, she shook her head.

"Let me." She rolled it over the length of him, then raised herself above him, her entire body quaking with desire. She wrapped her hand around the base of his erection and lowered herself, her eyes nearly rolling back at the intense pleasure of him filling her. Her inner muscles squeezed around him as she rocked back on her heels. His hands returned to her breasts, and she moved faster, wilder, a creature with no inhibitions. Their moans formed a frantic duet that bounced off the walls around them.

Distantly aware of the mattress squeaking, she reached for the headboard, using it for leverage as bright rapture spiraled through her. He gripped her waist, pumping into her fast and hard before finding his own release with a wordless shout.

Dani collapsed on top of him, limp and gloriously spent. She closed her eyes, waiting for her breath to even out and her heart rate to slow. Afterglow gradually ebbed into reality. She realized that she was parched, and that it was *really* hot in here.

"I'm going to get something to drink and adjust the air-conditioning." She gave him an apologetic smile. "And you should probably get dressed. Meg will be home soon."

"If she's not already. I don't know about you, but I wasn't paying a lot of attention to outside noise."

She felt a blush climb in her cheeks. Truthfully, there could have been a parade taking place in the next room, and she wouldn't have noticed. "I hope you understand why I'm not inviting you to stay over. The three of us, only the one master bath…it would be awkward." There was a superstitious part of her that whispered at least this way, she wouldn't wake up to any uncomfortable surprises.

"I have to be on-site at daybreak tomorrow anyway. If I slept over, I'd worry about disturbing you and Meg in the morning. But next time, we should do this at my place." He grinned. "I'll even get a multipack of tooth-brushes so you'll have your pick."

Next time. The words sent a thrill of anticipation through her that startled her. It was odd, feeling so anxious to see him again when he hadn't even left yet. But intuition told her making love with Sean wasn't a fleeting craving that could be satisfied. It was more like an addiction, growing stronger every time. If she weren't careful, she could lose herself in it.

It was too early Saturday morning for many people to be in the shop yet, and Meg was using the time to catch up on a few paperwork issues in the tiny office behind the cashier area. She was printing coupon flyers for a bra sale when Marissa let out a low whistle.

"I so hope the guy window-shopping comes into the store," her sister called to her. "He is— Good morning." Her formerly lascivious tone was now pure professionalism. "How can I help you?"

"Actually." A man cleared his throat. "I was looking for Meg."

Recognition of that deep voice kicked in, a fluttery feeling low in her belly. It had been several days since Dani said Bryce had asked about her, and Meg hadn't truly believed anything would come of it.

"Meg?" Marissa's tone was admirably casual, as if

movie-star-hot men came into the store all the time seeking her younger sister.

Meg wiped her suddenly clammy palms on the sides of her pants. The lime green capris and blue peasant blouse with matching lime ribbon accents were a far cry from country club garb. She'd twisted her curly hair in a knot at the back of her head, secured haphazardly by a pen she'd been using earlier.

Bryce, on the other hand, looked much the same as he had the last time she'd seen him. His hair was flawlessly styled, not a strand out of place, and he wore dark slacks with a crisp button-down shirt. This was his idea of Saturday morning wear? Didn't the guy own shorts or jeans?

Of course, given how devastatingly attractive and in charge he looked in his pressed clothes, why mess with a formula that worked?

"Hi," she said, hoping her smile didn't betray her nerves. "What brings you here?" Please Lord don't let him say he needed help finding something sexy for another woman.

"I, uh…" His gaze skittered to Marissa, who was folding camisoles on a nearby shelf. Though she wasn't looking at them, her curiosity was palpable. "Any chance I could buy you a cup of coffee?"

"Sure. I was due for a break anyway."

Bent over the camisole display, Marissa snorted. Meg had only arrived at work about thirty minutes ago. Her first regular break was hours away. But being co-owner had its benefits. Temporarily ditching the store to grab a latte with a gorgeous guy was one of them.

"There's a great coffee shop two doors down," Meg said. "Riss, I'll be back in a few minutes." Then she followed Bryce out the door. She imagined most women would happily follow him through the Sahara.

"I hope you don't mind my coming down here," he said, sounding almost shy. "I don't usually bother people at work for personal reasons. But I wanted to, ah, find out your last name."

He'd tracked her down early on a Saturday to ask her name? "Rafferty."

"Thank you. It seemed odd for me to ask a woman out when I didn't even know her full name."

She almost tripped over a nonexistent crack in the sidewalk. "You're asking me out?"

"That was the plan, yes."

His phrasing, along with years of cautionary advice from Dani, dimmed her immediate euphoria. Hadn't she just split up with a man who'd had her whole life planned out for her? Dani was always telling her she fell too hard, too fast. And if ever there was a guy who would tempt a girl to fall, it was Bryce Grayson.

"Um, what did you have in mind?" she asked as he held open the coffee shop door for her.

"I was hoping to take you to dinner."

Based on what she knew about him, it would probably be someplace classy. Which meant candlelight and a nice wine list. Bad idea.

"Maybe we could do that sometime," she said noncommittally. "But, in the meantime, how would you like to come to a cookout Dani and I are throwing?" It was an impulsive act of self-preservation. Surely her friend would understand. If Meg was going to avoid rushing headlong into another romantic folly, she needed to control the circumstances, make them less intimate.

Dani would be proud of her—if slightly vexed about the imaginary barbecue.

"That sounds wonderful. When is it?"

She had enough of a mental grip left not to say to-night. "Um, tomorrow. But I need to double-check the time with Dani. If you give me your number, I can text you."

She couldn't believe she'd just scored the hot guy's number and a date. If it weren't for the nagging concern that her best friend was going to kill her, Meg would be floating.

"You told him what?" Dani backed away from the stove, convinced she'd misheard over the sizzle of sesame oil she was heating for stir-fry.

"That we were having a cookout tomorrow and he's invited. I knew it would be what you wanted me to do."

Dani blinked at the blatant lack of logic in that statement. "Why would I want you to lie to him? I don't get your moral code." The woman who was staunchly opposed to uttering any four-letter words apparently had no problem with convenient fibs.

"He wanted to take me to dinner. I figured the two of us alone, over a nice meal, and I'd be putty in his hands. This way, I have you to smack me upside the head if I start getting too dewy-eyed. Please, Dani."

"Sean and I have plans. We're supposed to see that movie we never made it to last night." She couldn't imagine asking for a rain check for their rain check.

"If we eat early enough, you can still make it to one of the seven-thirty or eight o'clock showings," Meg pointed out. "I will do all the work. Let me buy the gro-ceries and cook dinner as a belated thank-you for giving me a place to crash. And if you're afraid the whole double date vibe will be awkward, I can invite Marissa and Ned. I'm sure they'd love a few kid-free hours."

"I don't know…" But she was weakening. It wasn't as though eating a hamburger before the movie was such a hardship.

Meg switched tactics. "Having dinner here first would give you even more time with Sean. You can't deny how much you enjoy his company. I saw the way you were beaming this morning."

Guilty. Normally, Dani didn't look forward to early morning house showings, especially on the weekend when most of the workforce was entitled to sleep in. But today, she'd rolled out of bed with a smile on her face and a song in her heart.

"You were practically *glowing*," Meg added. "If I weren't so happy for you, I'd be unbelievably jealous."

She couldn't deny that she was already looking forward to seeing Sean again. "I'll go to the main office and see if anyone's signed up to use the patio tomorrow," she relented. There were a few battered picnic tables and a community grill that tenants could reserve. "But this is awfully short notice. You may be out of luck."

"I don't think so." Meg's characteristically buoyant optimism was once again shining through. "Our luck is changing! You just have to be positive."

That attitude seemed simplistic, if not outright naive. In her last relationship, Dani had bought a wedding dress. Wasn't that being pretty damn positive? There were no guarantees.

Then again, Dani didn't allow defeatist thinking in her career. She approached each deal with confidence—

while simultaneously working her ass off to make sure she got the results she wanted. Perhaps she should approach dating with the same blend of self-assurance and strategy. If she wanted to avoid getting hurt again, it was up to her to make sure she didn't allow that possibility. *Have fun, but don't get too close.* No problem.

She smiled at Meg. "Maybe you're right. We make our own luck." As long as neither she nor Sean had unrealistic expectations, there was no reason they couldn't fully enjoy this affair.

ALEX PAUSED BY the watercooler in the trailer, staring in Sean's direction.

"Something wrong?" Sean asked. Sunday was their shortest shift, but they'd put in a productive day's work. Most everyone who'd clocked out in the past few minutes had been in high spirits.

"Do you realize you've been whistling for the past two days? It's starting to border on creepy. Being that happy ain't natural." His expression turned sly. "Let me guess. Did your mystery woman who wasn't interested change her mind?"

Am I really that transparent? Not that he cared. Let Alex or anyone else on the crew razz him. Time with Dani was worth any amount of mockery.

"Yeah, she did. In fact, I'm headed over to see her now." He'd been amused by her explanation that they were having an impromptu cookout, but that his brother wasn't supposed to know the impromptu part.

"Why, Ms. Yates," he'd teased over the phone, "surely you aren't asking me to participate in deception? I know you have very strong feelings about that."

She'd made a garbled noise that was part laugh and

part growl. "Just be here by four-thirty, and I'll owe you one."

He liked the sound of that.

Halfway across town, he caught sight of himself in his rearview mirror and realized he was grinning. Maybe Alex was right. Maybe being this happy wasn't natural. But, damn, it felt good.

He pulled up to Dani's building about the same time as Bryce. When he saw the familiar box in his brother's hand, he chuckled. "You and your imported beer."

"What's wrong with it?" Bryce asked. He eyed Sean's empty hands critically. "At least *I* brought a contribution."

Crap. He had a point. Sean had been so preoccupied with seeing her again—and trying to get here by four-thirty—that it hadn't occurred to him to stop for wine or flowers or any of the usual hostess offerings. *I'll make it up to her later.* That thought had him smiling again.

He knocked on the apartment door, and a woman he'd never seen before answered. From her freckles and vaguely familiar eyes, he guessed she was Meg's sister. She looked as though she was in her late-thirties, with just a touch of gray creeping into her strawberry-blond bob.

Her eyes were wide with surprise. "Well, hello there." Apparently, no one had warned her to expect identical twins. "I'm Marissa Talbot, Meg's sister." Her gaze darted between them before landing on Bryce, the brother with the more expensive clothes and conservative haircut. "I believe we've already met?"

She waved them through the apartment to a narrow backdoor that led to a cobblestone patio. Meg was standing at the grill, her cheeks rosy with heat. Dani stood off to the side, looking sexy as hell in a casual black halter dress. She was chatting with a guy in khakis who drank from a bottle of the same beer Bryce favored.

When Dani spotted Sean, her face lit up. But then she inexplicably scowled. Shaking off both expressions, she walked toward him. "Sean, Bryce, glad you two could join us! This is Meg's sister and brother-in-law, Marissa and Ned Talbot."

Bryce snapped his fingers. "Ned Talbot? From Humphrey Hall? I thought you looked familiar. Bryce Grayson. I lived in the dorm for a semester until I moved to the frat house."

"Right." Ned shook his hand, and the two men fell into discussing their mutual alma mater. It turned out Marissa had attended the same college, where she'd met her husband, but she'd lived clear on the other side of campus.

Standing at the grill, Meg chuckled. "Yeah, our parents trusted *her* to go to school out of state. Me, not so much. Which was probably a wise call," she added sheepishly.

Dani indicated the cooler of iced drinks sitting in the shade of a dilapidated picnic table. "You guys help yourself to whatever you want."

What Sean really wanted was a moment alone with her to greet her properly. From the way she wasn't quite meeting his eyes or stopping in his orbit for long, he guessed she wouldn't welcome a public display of affection. Well, they hadn't been dating long. Maybe being with him in front of her friends was an adjustment.

When she excused herself to go back inside for plates and condiments, he seized the opportunity for a moment alone and volunteered to assist. No sooner had they set foot in the apartment than he pulled her into his arms. After the barest hesitation, she melted against him, kissing him with the same welcome he'd glimpsed in her eyes when he first arrived. He hadn't consciously realized his shoulders were bunching with tension until they relaxed again.

"That was nice." She smiled up at him. "But we should probably get back out there."

"Okay. Later, though, I want you all to myself. Come home with me after the movie?" His words were a lot more patient than what he was thinking. *Come home with me now.*

She nodded eagerly. "I'd like that."

The genuine enthusiasm in her gaze as she smiled up at him was reassuring. Her earlier withdrawal must have been his imagination. *Quit overreacting.* The problem with being so happy was that, at times, it seemed too good to be true. Yet, when he touched her, it was obvious she wanted him as much as he did her—which made him a very lucky man.

She'd forgiven his lie, they'd met each other's families and she would be spending the night in his bed. What more could he ask for?

13

AFTER AN HOUR and a half of listening to the people around him share college stories—a topic Sean was ill-equipped to participate in—he was anxious to leave. He told the Talbots that it had been nice to meet them, a tactful fib he figured even Dani would pardon, then went inside to see if she was ready. Meg had excused herself to the kitchen to bring out dessert. Sean and Dani had declined, claiming that they were saving room for overpriced theater junk food.

Dani had been vehement. "An action movie without popcorn is like a football game with no goal posts."

Letting himself in through the backdoor, Sean heard Dani's voice from the kitchen. "You really don't have to keep thanking me," she said wryly.

"But I do! I'm grateful for today. And for letting me stay with you. For giving me your approval to see Bryce. It's funny that I like him so much, isn't it? He seems more your type. I guess your good taste in men is finally rubbing off on me."

Sean's jaw clenched, but he told himself to get over it. He'd known since day one that Dani had found Bryce attractive. That had been superficial, a few passing glances that were nothing compared to the hours she'd spent with Sean. *He* was the one who'd shot pool with her, danced with her at the country club, made love to her until they were both too spent to move. Ridiculous to be jealous over what-might-have-beens.

He cleared his throat more loudly than necessary, making his presence known.

Dani poked her head around the corner. "Just let me grab my purse." She disappeared into the bedroom and returned with a giant handbag.

He couldn't help laughing at its size. "Are you planning to smuggle in your own popcorn and soda?"

"No." She smirked. "It has some essential overnight gear, though. Like pajamas."

He raised an eyebrow. "Didn't I tell you? Dress code at my place is sleeping in the nude."

Her voice dropped to a husky whisper. "You might like these pajamas—they're from Meg's shop." She paused, tapping her index finger against her lips. "Although, strictly speaking, it's probably inaccurate to call a few scraps of black lace pajamas."

The visual images damn near shorted out his brain. So much for concentrating on the movie. "What about clothes for tomorrow?" he asked once he found his voice. "Are those crammed into your purse, too?" Which would be either really impressive or really scandalous. How small did a dress have to be to fit into a purse?

She laughed. "No, I'll come home to shower and change. I have a house showing scheduled in the morning before I head to the office, so I've got a little extra time."

He almost asked if she was sure she didn't want to

get ready at his place. It seemed more convenient. But at the thought of Dani in his shower, he suspected they'd both end up late for work.

THEY LEFT THE movie theater with differing opinions. "So you didn't like it?" Sean asked as he unlocked his SUV. He'd had a great time, although that could have been the company more than the film.

"I didn't exactly dislike it. I mean, I loved the first half. But when the villain took his girl Friday hostage and the hero realized he loved her? It got a little sappy for me."

"You have a problem with happy endings?" Sean teased.

"I… Maybe I question how happy they actually are. Or how the characters know they're with the right person."

"You just know." The words came out of nowhere, sounding incongruously serious for a conversation that had started with commentary on the hero's tights. He aimed for a more flippant tone. "I guess we'll have to wait for the sequel to see if they're still together."

Would he and Dani still be together by the time a sequel was released?

The thought was wildly unexpected. A follow-up movie was at least a year away. He'd never had a romantic relationship that had lasted that long. It wasn't even something he often considered. Yet he could easily imagine wanting Dani every bit as much one year from now as he did tonight. It was a foreign but not unpleasant feeling.

Dani didn't seem to mind his quiet introspection. As he drove, she turned up the radio, bopping along to some classic rock. It only took a few minutes to reach his town house.

He was renting from a man who'd invested heavily in real estate and had given Sean a good deal. In exchange for some minor repairs and carpentry to the townhomes the man owned on this block, Sean paid only about half the usual rent. It allowed him to live in a nicer place than he otherwise could have afforded. The floors weren't real hardwood, but they were a reasonable facsimile. Large windows helped create the illusion of space. The two-story townhome was nowhere near as luxurious as Bryce's loft, but it was sufficient for him. And preferable to Dani's small apartment.

"This is great," Dani said, dropping her purse on an end table and looking around. "I'm jealous."

He had the sudden mad impulse to give her a key and tell her she was welcome to visit any time. Or would that fall under her definition of too sappy?

"Hey." She poked him in the arm when he failed to respond, a teasing lilt in her voice. "You're not still thinking about the superhero's choice of crime-fighting ensemble, are you? Because if you're pondering his clothes instead of how to get me out of mine, I'm going to be deeply offended." She reached for his hand and led him to his favorite recliner, shoving playfully at his chest until he sat down.

"I wasn't thinking about superheroes. I was thinking about us," he admitted. "I've been doing that a lot."

Her smile faltered. "Oh?"

"All good things," he assured her. Scary good. Like, for the first time in his life he could understand how a couple could be married as long as his parents had been without getting tired of each other.

She perched on his lap. "There's definitely a time for thinking." Her fingers threaded through his hair, and she nipped at his lower lip. "But this feels like a time for doing."

That sounded like a philosophy he could support. Abandoning his awkward attempt at conversation, he lost himself in the pure, perfect pleasure of kissing her. Her tongue clashed with his, and lust shot through him. What was it about this woman that always had him teetering on the brink of need? A look, a touch, a kiss and suddenly getting his hands on her was as crucial as breathing.

He bunched up the material of her loose skirt, sliding his hands beneath the silky material, across her even silkier thighs. She squirmed atop him as if she weren't sure whether she wanted him to slow down or move faster.

He traced the outer edge of her ear with his tongue, loving how she melted against him. "Everything okay?"

"Everything's wonderful." She rocked against him for emphasis, and he sucked in a breath at the exquisite sensation. "It's just…when you touch me like that, I get distracted."

"Distracted from what? If you tell me you're trying to calculate mortgage rates, I'm going to stick my head in the oven."

She laughed. Then she braced her hands on the arms of the chair and pushed, unexpectedly getting to her feet. He immediately missed the contact.

"Wait, I take back the smart-ass comment," he said. "I—"

"Shush," she scolded playfully. "Do you want to know what you distracted me from or not?"

What he wanted was to haul her into the bedroom, but the wicked glint in her eyes was intriguing, so he kept quiet and let her continue.

"I have these thoughts. Actually, it's more accurate to call them fantasies." Her voice was velvet-wrapped sin, and he grew harder simply listening to her.

"Fantasies are good," he said hoarsely. Yay fantasies.

At the interruption, she shot him a stern look, but amusement danced in her gaze. "I think about things I want to do to you, things I plan to do, but then I get too caught up in how it feels when you touch me here." She slid her hand past the strap of her halter top, stopping when she reached the swell of her breast. Then her hand skated lower, temporarily disappearing between the loose folds of her skirt. "And here."

He forgot to breathe. Fully dressed, she was still the most erotic thing he'd ever seen. His voice was so strained it was barely recognizable in his own ears. "So if I promise not to, um, distract you…"

She gave him a grin of such devilish intent he doubted he would ever recover. "Well, that would leave me free to concentrate on other things." She hooked a finger through the belt loops on his jeans and tugged.

He scooted closer, to the edge of the chair, and she reached for the button. He was practically panting by the time she worked the zipper down and pulled him free. With the grace of a ballerina, she dropped to her knees between his legs. She raked her fingers over him, scraping lightly with her nails just enough to make him hiss in conflicted pleasure.

Then she leaned down and closed her lips over him, drawing him into the indescribable bliss of her mouth.

An almost brutal ecstasy sizzled through him, incinerating coherent thought.

Within minutes, he'd forgotten his own name. But hers rolled off his lips over and over like a mantra.

DANI SHIFTED IN her seat, trying to focus on what Renee was saying about lending limits for homebuyers. But Dani was having a difficult time with mind over body today. Last night, Sean had made love to her with a pounding ferocity, as if he couldn't get close enough, as if he needed to make himself part of her. She wasn't exactly sore this morning, but there were enough physical twinges to keep him at the forefront of her mind.

"Did I lose you?" Renee asked, sounding surprised. Dani had never been one for daydreaming.

"Sorry. I was just making a mental note that I need to call Sean Andersen today." When her employer's eyebrows shot upward, Dani realized her mistake. "Ross! Ross Andersen."

Renee rose from the chair on the other side of Dani's desk. "Well, make sure you get your head together before you call him."

"Yes. Absolutely. Will do." Dani couldn't have been more mortified if she'd been caught doodling little hearts with Sean's name in them. So they'd had an intensely passionate night—it hadn't been the first one they'd shared. Nor did it change the effort she owed her clients. *And myself.*

When her phone rang, she reached for it eagerly, determined to sound her most professional. But it was Sean's number on the screen. It annoyed her how happy she was to see it there. "Hello?"

There was a pause, no doubt due to her irritated tone. "Rough day?" he asked carefully.

"Sorry. You caught me at a bad time."

"Want to talk about it?" he offered, making her feel even worse for the way she'd snapped her greeting.

"Thanks, but no. I'm just a little behind and need to kick it into gear."

"Then I'll make this quick. Some of us are planning to go bowling tonight. I remembered that you used to bowl and thought you might like to join us. At least one of the other guys is bringing his wife."

"Tonight?" They'd seen each other as recently as that morning. And she hadn't gone an hour without thinking about him since driving away from his place. Spending a second consecutive night with him didn't seem conducive to her plan of moving slow and not getting overly attached.

When her silence began stretching into awkwardness, he added, "I just thought I'd toss it out there in case you weren't busy tonight. No big deal. If you decide you want to join us, text me later." Something about the way he tried to make the invitation sound casual made it even less so.

"Okay." Her innate sense of honesty prompted her to add, "But I don't think I'll make it." The bigger question was, what about the next time he called?

How long was an appropriate amount of time to go between seeing him so that she could reassure herself that the relationship wasn't getting serious? And what would happen when she could no longer believe that?

THE CRASH OF bowling balls thundering into pins had become white noise, a distant background to Sean's thoughts as he awaited his turn. Jacob and his wife stood by the ball return, affectionately heckling each other. Alex had gone for a pitcher of soda and, with any luck, the bartender's phone number. Sean was lost in mental replays of his phone conversation with Dani today. She'd sounded...strained.

He'd never been a paranoid person. With the exception of his competitive streak, he was fairly easygoing. But first there'd been the weird distance at her cookout, which he had tried to chalk up to his overactive imagination and feeling out of place among her college-educated friends. Then today—

"When I told you the cheerful whistling was getting creepy," Alex said, setting a pitcher and a stack of plastic glasses on the table, "I didn't mean you should take up brooding. Find some middle ground, dude."

"Sorry." He poured himself a soda. "How'd it go with the bartender?"

"She remembered me from last time I was here and seemed glad to see me. Victory is imminent."

Sean made a skeptical noise.

"You doubt my skills with the ladies?"

"No. But 'the ladies' can be unpredictable."

"No kidding. I have sisters, remember?" Alex nodded toward the lane. "You're up."

Sean knocked down eight pins but missed the split. Alex got nine, then threw a gutter ball trying to pick up the spare. Jacob's wife got the first strike of the game and smirked at the men. It was a shame Dani hadn't come—she'd like Maria.

"Okay, seriously." Alex slugged him in the arm. "What the hell? You're depressing me. What zapped your good mood? I thought you won the girl."

So did I.

"Are you two fighting?" Alex asked.

"No." They'd had one hell of an intense night last night, but it hadn't included any arguing. "I just think something's on her mind."

"Try asking her about it. According to my sisters, 'communication is key.'" He punctuated this advice with air-quotes and a falsetto voice. "It sucks, but if you like her, you might actually have to talk about the Relationship."

Sean would have chuckled at his friend's ominous tone if he weren't so perplexed. "Actually, I tried to talk to her about the relationship last night. But we, um, got distracted."

"You dog." Alex looked impressed. When Sean didn't return his smile, he shook his head. "Hold up— you're *unhappy* because your girl would rather do the mattress mambo than discuss her feelings? That's like the holy grail of relationships right there!"

There was a time Sean might have believed that. As he rose to take his next turn, he questioned why he felt so discontent. Dani was a fun, sexy woman who wasn't pressing him to do more with his life or analyze their every interaction. Why wasn't that enough? When did he get greedy for more?

When I started falling in love with her.

BY THE TIME Dani got the text asking if Sean could cook her dinner Wednesday, she was desperate to see him again. Meg had babysat one of her nephews on Monday and gone out with Bryce on Tuesday, leaving Dani plenty of solitary hours to think about Sean, replaying favorite snippets of conversation in her head and reliving the feel of his body moving against hers.

She knocked on his front door, flutters of anticipation quickening in her abdomen. He answered immediately, barefoot in a pair of dark jeans and wearing an untucked button-down shirt with a plaid dishtowel thrown over his shoulder.

A grin spread across his face. "Hello, beautiful." He plucked at the leather strap of her small purse. "Any chance you're carrying another set of interesting 'pajamas' in there?" The black lace had been a hit. He'd told her she was stunning in the garment, then promptly ripped it off her.

"No pajamas necessary. I have an early morning, so I won't be staying the night." His expression was so crestfallen, she hastily added, "But I promise you'll like what I'm wearing under the suit. Unless you aren't in favor of thongs?" she added coyly.

With a growl, he tugged her against him. His tongue delved into her mouth with such possessive sensuality that she trembled. He slid his hands over the fabric of her suit skirt, palming her butt. He didn't break their kiss until an insistent beeping sounded from the kitchen.

"Oven timer," he said ruefully. "I've worked too hard pretending I can cook to let dinner burn."

"Well, whatever you're pretending to cook smells wonderful," she said, catching the aroma of some kind of red-wine sauce. As she followed him toward the kitchen, she spotted candles on the table. Between two pillars sat a flower arrangement that was an exact match of the one he'd sent to her office.

She was caught off guard by the romantic touches.

"There's no fairy in this one." The observation was the first thing she could think of to say.

"No." He gave her a lopsided smile, full of charm. "She was one of a kind. I checked the chicken, and it still needs time. Can I pour you some wine?"

"Yes, please."

He pulled a bottle of chardonnay from the refrigerator and filled the two glasses that sat on the counter, handing one to her. "I asked Bryce to suggest a bottle, so it should be excellent."

First the flowers, now expensive wine? In the years she'd dated Tate, he'd only gone out of his way to cook for her once—the night he'd proposed. Déjà vu thudded to the pit of her stomach like a rock. "What's the occasion?"

"You," he said, raising his glass as if toasting her.

His simple declaration left her divided. There was the Dani who was utterly beguiled by the sincerity in his voice, who wanted to repay his thoughtfulness by covering him in kisses. Then there was the Dani who recoiled, afraid that her plan of keeping an emotional safety net was failing. To keep from saying anything ungrateful, she took a healthy slug of wine.

"So how's Meg doing?" he asked. "Fully recovered from her breakup?"

"She certainly seemed chipper enough when your brother picked her up last night." On the one hand, Dani questioned whether her friend had allowed sufficient recovery time before throwing herself into her next romantic involvement. But on the other hand, Nolan didn't deserve Meg's pining, and Bryce seemed to be treating her well. *Don't they all, at first?*

Dani cleared her throat. "She, um, found a place to live, but she can't move in until the first of next month."

"Well, if your apartment ever feels cramped, you're always welcome here," he said. She must have paled or made a face because his eyes suddenly narrowed. "What? I thought you liked it here?"

"I do."

"Yet I can barely convince you to stay the night. And sometimes when I suggest we spend time together, you give me that look."

"What look?"

"The 'back off, buddy' look that I'm getting right now."

"We did agree to take this slowly," she said defensively.

He set his wineglass down on the counter hard enough to make the liquid inside slosh wildly. "Slow isn't the same as stagnant. We spent the night together on our first date. At some point, don't you think there's a natural progression from there?"

"T-to what?" she asked, scared to know the answer. Living together? Marriage? Inevitable heartbreak?

"I don't know." He shoved a hand through his hair. "To a place where I can suggest you bring a curling iron over and get ready for work here without you freaking out and pushing me away."

"I…" She instinctively wanted to deny his words, but the truth was, she thought this would work better with some degree of distance. "I'm not thinking in terms of curling irons and your giving me drawer space. I was just looking for fun."

The words, which had previously seemed harmless,

now rang hollow. Almost cruel. Sean sucked in a breath, his eyes hurt.

He laughed, and it was a harsh sound, full of disbelief and contempt. "You're a lot like my last girlfriend, you know that? She thought I was fun, too. *A good time.* Those were her exact words. Not a legitimate prospect for ever sharing her life with, but a talented lay for sharing her bed."

"That's not fair!" She didn't know what sickened her more—that he might actually see himself like that or that he could somehow believe she did.

"No, what isn't fair is falling for a woman who…" He looked bleakly past her, at the immaculately set table, then met her eyes. "I'm not looking for something as shallow as fun. I want more than that. I deserve more than that," he said quietly.

Her eyes burned with frustration and unshed tears. She was furious with herself for ruining the nice dinner he'd planned and furious with him for pushing for more than she could give. It had been simpler when they were two strangers shooting pool, interested in a little hot sex with no strings.

"You knew when I met you," she said softly, "that I wasn't looking for a relationship. I wasn't looking for roses or commitment or fancy wine."

"You think I was?" He glanced away, his lips twisting in a sad smile. "I was not looking for you, Danica Yates. And finding you has been something of a mixed blessing. I think you should probably go."

"What?" The unexpected rejection sent her reeling. She waved her hand in a vague gesture, trying to encompass both the table behind them and the food that was still cooking. "But you went to all this work."

"Yeah," he agreed sadly. "I worked hard to get you to forgive me, to get you to go out with me. I'm done now. The truth is, you can't give me what I need."

"Are you...breaking up with me?" she asked, feeling a little lost.

"I'm not sure you can call it that. Breaking up implies we had a real relationship to begin with." He said it with more regret than anger, and she almost wished he was yelling. Fighting would be easier than this remorse bubbling up inside her like acid. She'd hurt him.

Her vision swam, and she knew she had to get out of here if she didn't want him to see her cry. But she couldn't leave him thinking that he'd been no more to her than a random sexual partner. "Sean, you have to know that...I care about you." The words came out stiff and flat, not doing her emotions justice.

"The fact that you can barely admit that much is why we shouldn't see each other again." He took a step forward, moving close just long enough to drop a kiss to her forehead. "Goodbye, Dani."

WHEN THE DOOR to the apartment opened, Meg and Bryce sprang apart in surprise. *Shoot.* Meg had been so sure he was about to kiss her for the first time. Why was Dani back so soon? Meg hadn't expected her home for hours.

She rose from the couch, not meeting Bryce's gaze for fear a blush would flame across her face. She'd *really* wanted him to kiss her. "Forget your cell phone or something?" she called to her roommate.

Dani's face was pale, her eyes stricken. "Or something."

Meg's heart sank. "You guys had a fight?"

"He told me to go. He said…" Her gaze briefly lit on Bryce, then flitted away as if looking at him was painful. "Never mind, you two carry on. I'm going to bed early and won't be a bother to anyone."

Meg turned back to her date. "Sorry, but I have to kick you out now."

He squeezed her shoulder. "I'd expect no less. You're a loyal and compassionate woman." He leaned forward and brushed the lightest kiss across the corner of her mouth. "You're also incredibly sexy, but we'll discuss that another time."

Her heart thudded in giddy pleasure and as he turned to go, she grabbed him by the lapels of his suit jacket and planted a kiss soundly on his lips, letting herself melt into it for the briefest of moments, her mouth opening eagerly beneath his as she breathed in the scent of him, the warmth of him.

"Right, then." She patted him on the chest, happy to see her basic motor functions were still functioning. A kiss like that could shock a girl's system. "Call me soon."

"Tomorrow," he promised, his gorgeous eyes looking a bit dazed. "And I wouldn't even wait that long except I think your friend needs you."

"You should know, I warned your brother that if he hurt her, I would end him. How would you feel about being an only child?"

Bryce chuckled. "There have been days when it was my fondest wish." But then he sobered. "I have to say, though, it's hard to imagine him hurting her. The way he looks at her? I would have bet money he was a man in love."

She grimaced, knowing Dani's feelings on that subject. "For his sake, I hope not."

WHEN DANI CAME home from a closing the following Monday afternoon, she was surprised to find Meg sitting in her living room. She hadn't seen much of her friend since rather rudely stonewalling Meg last week, claiming she had no intention of discussing her breakup with Sean and wasn't interested in anyone's opinion on the subject.

Dani was even more surprised to see that her unused wedding gown was draped over the living room sofa. "What on earth are you doing with that?"

"I needed a visual aid." Meg's eyes were gleaming and her arms were crossed. She looked like someone prepared for battle. "Do you remember the day we went shopping for a dress? You had a checklist of practical considerations, like budget and the usual weather conditions for the month you were getting married."

"Yeah. I planned ahead. I do that."

"Yes, very practical of you. And you found a dress that fit you well and matched all your criteria."

Dani nodded, lamenting the wasted time and money. "The perfect dress."

"No." Meg shook her finger at her. "Because you didn't *love* the dress. You didn't light up when you looked in the mirror with that 'yes, this is the one!' bridal glow. And you approached your relationship with Tate in much the same way. He made sense according to some sort of practical boyfriend list you had in your head. But he didn't make you glow."

Dani ground her teeth in frustration. "Not everyone's as emotionally open as you are, Rafferty. I'm not a very glowy person." Nor did she want to be. It was a silly basis for long-term decisions. "You think I tell my clients to buy houses based on which ones give them the goofiest smiles when they walk through the door? There are inspections to schedule and lenders to consult."

"I don't think you give your heart enough credit," Meg argued. "You think that just because it's an emotional decision, it can't also be intelligent? Your heart was smart enough not to fall in love with Tate Malcom. He didn't deserve you. I think Sean Grayson does. And what's more, you think that, too. Your heart's shouting it at you, and you're being a pansy. You've been miserable all week in a sterile, I-refuse-to-cry, emotionless-robot kind of way. He made you happy!"

Sometimes. He also made her nervous. She realized now that Tate had been safe. On some level, she'd known even when she agreed to marry him that there was no chance he'd ever break her heart the way her mother's death had broken her father's. Sean was exhilarating and consuming and dangerous. He would never be "safe."

Because she couldn't contest Meg's point, she limited her response to a stiff, "I didn't ask your opinion."

Meg snorted. "That's never stopped you from giving yours. And most of your advice to me has been spot-on. Well, it's my turn now. *I'm* the one with the good advice. But it's up to you to get your head out of your ass and take it!"

Dani blinked. "Did you just swear at me?"

"You're damn right I did! Extenuating circumstances. I've never seen you truly in love before, and I can't stand that you let it slip through your fingers."

"It's not like *I* broke up with *him*," Dani protested. "He said he didn't want to see me again."

"And you didn't fight to change his mind? That's

what he would have done. That's what he did do. Because he thought you were worth it."

Dani's throat burned and it was tough to get the words out. "Maybe he was wrong." She'd called him "fun," as if he was a day at an amusement park. He deserved someone who could love him back, and she wasn't sure she was that person.

14

AN HOUR LATER, Dani pulled into the parking lot of an upscale sports bar. Meg had left because she had plans with her sister, and Dani couldn't stand to be alone in her own company right now. Plus, that damn wedding dress had been mocking her, taunting her with plans that hadn't come to fruition and a future she might never have.

Wanting an excuse to flee her apartment that didn't feel cowardly, she'd called Erik Frye. There was a baseball game on tonight, and she'd suggested they watch it together and grab some dinner. She knew he was still worried about his mother and figured they could both use some distraction.

He was already inside, having come straight from work. The sports bar was around the corner from his office. He hailed her from a back corner booth. The spicy smell of buffalo wings was prevalent. On any other day, her stomach would have rumbled in expectation.

"The waitress already brought our waters out," he said, pushing a plate of lemon wedges toward her. He'd once teased that with the amount of citrus she put in her water, she should just order lemonade. "But on the phone you sounded like you might need something stronger to drink."

"I don't know what I need." Maybe the number of a good therapist. "A friendly shoulder?"

"You got it. I can just listen or give actual advice. Unless it's legal advice," he teased. "Then I have to bill you."

She managed a wan smile. "I've already had more advice than I can stand today. But it didn't solve my problem."

"I'm guessing this problem is a man?"

I don't know. She was starting to think *she* was her problem. "Can I ask you a question about your marriage?"

"Fire away. But since it ended in divorce, I can hardly claim to be an expert."

"That's my question." She fiddled with the straw in her drink. She wasn't thirsty for her usual lemon water today. The taste in her mouth was bitter enough. "If you'd known how it would go, that you and your wife would get divorced, would you still have married her? That sounds stupid, doesn't it? Of course you wouldn't—"

"Actually, I would." He looked surprised by his own admission. "We had a lot of good years before things took a wrong turn, and I wouldn't trade those for anything."

Though she hadn't asked her father the question— she hesitated bringing up his wife's death—she knew deep down his answer would be the same. He wouldn't have sacrificed the time he had with Gina. "My dad's a widower," she said. "I don't know if I ever told you that. I don't really remember my mom, but she was the love of his life."

"Must've been hard on him to lose her."

"I'm not sure he's ever been the same. He still misses her, still loves her. It seems a rather tragic way to live."

He raised an eyebrow. "Tell me the truth, is your calling me here tonight really my secretary's idea? Because this sounds like a very subtle intervention."

She laughed out loud. "I'm not hinting that you're tragic. Trust me."

"Good. I hope to get over my wife, eventually. I don't think failed love dooms you to be alone forever. I can't know what your father's going through, exactly, but we make choices. I choose to believe that having loved Margot makes me a better person and that maybe I learned from my mistakes and will have better relationships in the future. I'm not ready yet, but that doesn't mean I'll never be."

I'm not ready yet. That's what she should have told Sean. She should have embraced what he said about evolving. He hadn't asked her to love him right now, he'd only asked that she give the possibility a chance. And she'd resisted to the point of losing him.

"No." Bryce Grayson scanned the hallway nervously as if searching for exit options. But to get to the elevator, he would have to get past Dani. "Meg said you might come to me seeking help, but the answer is no."

In the week since Dani's dinner with Erik, she'd done a lot of thinking. About Sean. About love. About being braver and trusting her heart. But since Sean wasn't returning her phone calls, she hadn't had much chance to tell him. She'd shown up at the Magnolia Grove site once, ambushing him the way he had in her office so long ago, but he'd said there was a foundation emergency that required his attention. Then he'd told her Alex could answer any questions she had about the housing development.

Alex's sympathetic eyes and soft "give him time" were kind but hadn't made her feel any better. It had been Meg's suggestion that they ask Bryce for help, but he was proving uncooperative. If there was a silver lining in any of this, it seemed to be that Bryce and Sean were closer than they'd been in years.

"I know you don't want to be disloyal to your brother," she said, "and I applaud that. But I'm having a hard time getting through to him."

"Oh, you got through to him. You wrecked him. Guys have a lot of pride," he said. "He put himself out there—"

"Bryce." She held up a hand. "I love your brother. I am going to tell him that with or without your help, but I'd like to do it in a way that doesn't involve my leaving it in a voice mail or in front of an audience. He said once that you didn't understand why he kept fighting for me, why he didn't just give up. But he was stubborn."

The corner of his mouth kicked up in a reluctant grin. "Always has been."

"Well, I am equally stubborn. It's one of the things that is going to make us a great match. Now that I've, um…"

"Pulled your head out of your ass?" he supplied, eyes dancing with humor.

"Meg mentioned that, huh?" She smiled back at him, feeling a burgeoning sense of camaraderie. "Bryce. Please. If you can help me get five minutes alone with him, I can say what I need to. After that, if he decides…" She blinked furiously. The past week and a half without him had sucked too tremendously to contemplate his continued absence from her life.

Bryce considered her plea. "Around a month ago, my brother got help sneaking into a locked room to leave me a gift. It occurs to me now," he said mischievously, "that I never returned the favor."

FRANKLY, SEAN DIDN'T want to go home, but after Alex and several other friends all canceled plans at the last minute, he couldn't think of where else to go. He wasn't stupid enough to go drinking without a designated driver, he lacked the charm and energy to flirt with women and he was avoiding his parents, not ready to tell his mom he'd broken up with Dani. He'd tried calling Bryce, who'd been surprisingly supportive lately, but his brother hadn't answer the phone. No doubt his twin was canoodling somewhere with Meg.

A sharp pain twisted inside as Sean unlocked his front door. He was screwed if Bryce and Meg got married, because he couldn't see her or think about her without being reminded of Dani. Of course, working in the Magnolia Grove subdivision also reminded him of Dani. Maybe he needed a mini vacation somewhere out of her daily sphere. Like the Yukon.

He knew she'd tried calling him, but he didn't trust himself to pick up the phone. He was caught between wanting more than she had to offer yet doubting he could resist her if she tried to seduce him. He stepped inside the town house, surprised by the spill of light from upstairs. He didn't remember leaving that on, but he'd been in a preoccupied haze. Maybe that was why

Alex's plans had suddenly—and unconvincingly—altered; Sean was such an easy mark that it wasn't even fun to beat him at pool these days.

But then Dani appeared at the railing that overlooked the first floor. He stared hard, seriously hoping he wasn't hallucinating. He didn't think he was *that* far gone.

"Sean." She made his name an endearment, and he regretted ever telling her to call him Gray. That was for people like Alex. The casual nickname was far too impersonal for this woman who'd wrung out his heart.

"How did you get in here?" It was the simplest question. He wasn't ready to voice his others.

"Your brother said to tell you that turnabout is fair play. Are you coming up, or should I come down?" she asked, trying to sound in charge. Even from this distance, her vulnerability was unmistakable. She was afraid of being hurt. If she'd been less afraid, they could have had something special together.

He shook his head. "I should probably turn around and leave."

"Well, it's your place. You'd have to come back eventually. And there's something up here I want to show you."

"If it's rose petals on the bed or something lacy from Meg's shop, you should know I'm not sleeping with you." He was glad he sounded more resolute than he felt. Because, damn, she looked good in that green wrap dress, her hair spilling over her shoulders in untamed waves.

She flinched at the verbal rejection. "It's not rose petals or anything lacy," she promised solemnly. "I'm here to talk, not lure you into bed."

Yet she wanted him to come to the bedroom for this little chat? Filled with suspicion, he went up the stairs. As he got closer, he noticed the shimmer in her eyes and recalled Meg warning him not to make her cry. That had never been his intention. He'd wanted to spoil Dani rotten. He'd wanted to satisfy her every sexual need and pamper her with attention outside the bedroom. She made him want to be chivalrous, unless they were in a pool hall. He respected her enough as an opponent to kick her ass without holding back.

"I miss you," she said huskily.

He missed her, too, with an unparalleled ache. He could bash his thumb with a hammer repeatedly and never achieve the kind of pain she'd caused.

"I'm sorry I wasn't more gracious about the dinner you cooked me," she began. "I'd love to make it up to you. But more important, I'm sorry I didn't trust us. You said once that trust was earned. You've been there for me, winning my trust, winning my heart. And I didn't think I was ready for that."

The words were a balm to his pride, but he'd spent weeks trying to woo this woman. A guy could only get rejected so many times before learning his lesson. "I know you've been through a lot. Losing your mom." Even if she didn't remember her, she'd had to deal with the aftermath of her father's loss. "That idiot Malcom cheating on you. Me lying to you. So I get it, intellectually. But I can't sit around hoping you feel differently someday, being your diversion in the meantime."

She reached out to grab his hand, and the sweet familiarity of her touch went through him like a shock. "You were always more than a diversion. The first night together, even when I thought you were someone else,

I wondered how I'd face you again in a platonic way. I may have been looking for casual sex, but there was nothing casual about what we shared. Not ever."

When she turned and led him toward the bedroom, he wasn't sure he should believe her claim of only being here to talk. That thought filled him with more excitement than it should.

Hadn't he promised never to lie to her again? "Dani, I want you. So damn badly. But I'm not happy about it."

She actually grinned. "I remember feeling exactly like that. I forgave you. I'm hoping you can do me the same courtesy."

To his surprise, she didn't go anywhere near the big king bed. Instead, she turned toward the bathroom. If she offered to live out any of his shower fantasies about the two of them, he was toast.

She stopped in the doorway, glancing nervously from him into the room. He followed her gaze. On the marbled vanity, his things had all been moved to one side. On the other side of the sink were cosmetics, a toothbrush and a curling iron.

"I brought some things over," she said shyly. "Like you suggested. There's a book I'm reading in the living room and some fresh lemons in the kitchen. Obviously you can tell me it's too late. You can kick me out, but I'm not telling you where all my stuff is," she threatened, gaining confidence. Or at least bravado.

"You'll run across a ceramic fairy on a shelf or my favorite nightshirt tucked into a drawer somewhere and you'll miss me. I know how horrible that feels because I've been missing you every single day. I want to spare you that. Because I…" Her lower lip quivered, and her eyes glistened. She lifted her chin. "Because I love—"

He claimed her mouth in a scorching kiss. Later, he wanted to hear her say it, that she loved him. Over and over, preferably when he was inside her. But for now, he couldn't wait any longer to kiss her, couldn't let her wonder any longer if he would forgive her or send her away. *Never.* Her body was plastered against his, her breath ragged as his hands roved her curves.

He broke off their kiss but didn't lift his head, saying the words against her lips. A different kind of kissing. "I love you, too."

Her hold on him tightened, and she swallowed convulsively, battling back tears. But her smile was full of sly mischief. "Then can I admit that I actually *am* wearing something lacy under this, picked out just for you? I should warn you, it's kind of complicated, though."

Scooping her up, he strode toward the bed. "That's okay." He smirked. "I've always been pretty talented with my hands."

He would happily spend hours demonstrating that. But he would spend years demonstrating how good he was with his heart.

* * * * *

COMING NEXT MONTH FROM

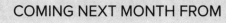

HARLEQUIN

Blaze

Available April 21, 2015

#843 A SEAL'S PLEASURE
Uniformly Hot!
by Tawny Weber
Tessa Monroe is used to men falling at her feet, but Gabriel Thorne is the first one to kiss his way back up to her heart. Can this SEAL's pleasure last, or will their fling end in tears?

#844 INTRIGUE ME
It's Trading Men!
by Jo Leigh
Lisa Cassidy is a PI with a past and Daniel McCabe is the sexy doc she's investigating. But everything changes after an unexpected and sizzling one-night stand...

#845 THE HOTTEST TICKET IN TOWN
The Wrong Bed
by Kimberly Van Meter
Laci McCall needs to lie low for a while so she goes home to Kentucky. She doesn't expect to end up in bed with Kane Dalton—her first love and the man who broke her heart.

#846 OUTRAGEOUSLY YOURS
by Susanna Carr
To revamp her reputation, Claire Miller pretends to have a passionate affair with notorious bachelor Jason Strong. But when their fling becomes a steamy reality, Claire can't tell what's true and what is only fantasy.

REQUEST YOUR FREE BOOKS!
2 FREE NOVELS PLUS 2 FREE GIFTS!

red-hot reads!

Tessa Monroe looked at the group of men who'd just walked in.

Her heart raced and emotions spun through her, too fast to identify.

"Why is he… Are they here?" she asked her friend Livi.

"The team? You don't think Mitch would celebrate our engagement without his SEALs, do you?" Livi asked as she waved them over.

As one, the men looked their way.

But Tessa only saw one man.

Taller than the rest, his shoulders broad and tempting beneath a sport coat the same vivid black as his eyes, he managed to look perfectly elegant.

His gaze locked on her, sending a zing of desire through her body with the same intensity as it had the first time he'd looked her way months before.

Tessa Monroe, the woman who always came out on top when it came to the opposite sex, wanted to hide.

"That's so sweet of his friends to come all this way to celebrate your engagement," she said, watching Livi's fiancé stride through the crowd to greet the group.

"They're all based in Coronado now. Didn't I tell you?" Livi asked, her eyes locked on Mitch as if she could eat him up. "Romeo's the best man."

Romeo.

Tessa's smile dropped away as dread and something else curled low in her belly.

Gabriel Thorne. Aka, Romeo.

His eyes were still locked on her and Tessa could see the heat in that midnight gaze.

It was as if he could look inside her mind, deep into her soul—and see everything. All of her desires, her every need, her secret wants.

A wicked smile angled over his chiseled face, assuring her he not only saw them all, but that he was also quite sure that he could fulfill every single one. And in ways that would leave her panting, sweaty and begging for more.

There was very little Tessa didn't know about sex. She appreciated the act, reveled in the results and had long ago mastered the ins and outs of, well, in and out. She knew how to use sex, how to enjoy sex and how to avoid sex.

So if anyone had told her that she'd feel a low, needy promise of an orgasm curling tight in her belly from just a single look across a crowded room, she'd have laughed at them.

Don't miss
A SEAL'S PLEASURE by Tawny Weber,
available May 2015 wherever
Harlequin® Blaze® books and ebooks are sold.

www.Harlequin.com

JUST CAN'T GET ENOUGH?

Join our social communities
and talk to us online.

You will have access to the latest
news on upcoming titles and special
promotions, but most importantly,
you can talk to other fans about your
favorite Harlequin reads.

Harlequin.com/Community

Facebook.com/HarlequinBooks

Twitter.com/HarlequinBooks

Pinterest.com/HarlequinBooks

HARLEQUIN®

A Romance FOR EVERY MOOD™

Stay up-to-date on all your
romance-reading news with the
Harlequin Shopping Guide,
featuring bestselling authors, exciting new
miniseries, books to watch and more!

The newest issue will be delivered right to you
with our compliments! There are 4 each year.

Signing up is easy.

EMAIL

ShoppingGuide@Harlequin.ca

WRITE TO US

HARLEQUIN BOOKS
Attention: Customer Service Department
P.O. Box 9057, Buffalo, NY 14269-9057

OR PHONE

1-800-873-8635 in the United States
1-888-343-9777 in Canada

Please allow 4-6 weeks for delivery of the first issue by mail.

THE WORLD IS BETTER WITH

Romance

Harlequin has everything from contemporary, passionate and heartwarming to suspenseful and inspirational stories.

Whatever your mood, we have a romance just for you!